ARE YOU B̲.̲.̲.̲.̲ᴳ SERVED?

A Play

by Jeremy Lloyd and David Croft

⫴SAMUEL FRENCH⫼

samuelfrench.co.uk

ISBN 978-0-573-01963-0
www.samuelfrench.co.uk
www.samuelfrench.com

For Amateur Production Enquiries

United Kingdom and World
excluding north america
plays@samuelfrench.co.uk
020 7255 4302/01

Each title is subject to availability from Samuel French,
depending upon country of performance.

THINKING ABOUT PERFORMING A SHOW?

There are thousands of plays and musicals available to perform from Samuel French right now, and applying for a licence is easier and more affordable than you might think

From classic plays to brand new musicals, from monologues to epic dramas, there are shows for everyone.

Plays and musicals are protected by copyright law, so if you want to perform them, the first thing you'll need is a licence. This simple process helps support the playwright by ensuring they get paid for their work and means that you'll have the documents you need to stage the show in public.

Not all our shows are available to perform all the time, so it's important to check and apply for a licence before you start rehearsals or commit to doing the show.

LEARN MORE & FIND THOUSANDS OF SHOWS

Browse our full range of plays and musicals, and find out more about how to license a show
www.samuelfrench.co.uk/perform

Talk to the friendly experts in our Licensing team for advice on choosing a show and help with licensing
plays@samuelfrench.co.uk   020 7387 9373

Acting Editions

BORN TO PERFORM

Playscripts designed from the ground up to work the way you do in rehearsal, performance and study

---

Larger, clearer text for easier reading

Wider margins for notes

Performance features such as character and props lists, sound and lighting cues, and more

---

+ CHOOSE A SIZE AND STYLE TO SUIT YOU

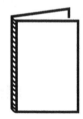

STANDARD EDITION

Our regular paperback book at our regular size

SPIRAL-BOUND EDITION

The same size as the Standard Edition, but with a sturdy, easy-to-fold, easy-to-hold spiral-bound spine

LARGE EDITION

A4 size and spiral bound, with larger text and a blank page for notes opposite every page of text – perfect for technical and directing use

LEARN MORE | samuelfrench.co.uk/actingeditions

Other plays by JEREMY LLOYD AND DAVID CROFT
published and licensed by Samuel French

'Allo 'Allo

Dad's Army

FIND PERFECT PLAYS TO PERFORM AT
www.samuelfrench.co.uk/perform

ARE YOU BEING SERVED?

Presented on stage at the Winter Gardens, Blackpool, with the following cast of characters:

MR GRAINGER	Larry Noble
MR MASH	Stewart Sherwin
MR RUMBOLD	Nicholas Smith
MR LUCAS	Michael Mundell
MISS BRAHMS	Wendy Richard
CAPTAIN PEACOCK	Frank Thornton
MRS SLOCOMBE	Mollie Sugden
MR HUMPHRIES	John Inman
MR GRACE	A.S.M.
LADY CUSTOMER	Barbara Rosenblat
MALE CUSTOMER	Raymond Bowers
NURSE	A.S.M.
DON BERNARDO	Stewart Sherwin
CESAR	Raymond Bowers
CONCHITA	Petra Siniawski
TAERESA	Barbara Rosenblat

The play was directed by **Roger Redfarn**

CHARACTERS

MR GRAINGER
MR MASH / doubling DON BERNARDO or CESAR
MR RUMBOLD
MR LUCAS
MISS BRAHMS
CAPTAIN PEACOCK
MRS SLOCOMBE
MR HUMPHRIES
LADY CUSTOMER / doubling TAERESA
MALE CUSTOMER / doubling DON BERNARDO or CESAR
NURSE / doubling CONCHITA
MR GRACE /ASM

The action of the play takes place on the shop floor of the Grace Brothers department store and at the Don Bernardo Hotel in Spain

PRODUCTION NOTES
Prepared by David Croft

Bavarian Dance

Any three/four oom pah pah Germanic music will do. In the TV show, according to my records, we used a piece called "In Munchen Steht ein Hofbrauhaus Ms 10142F – German Dance Music".

Chattering Teeth effect

This requires some ingenuity! We took advantage of a talented enthusiast at the BBC special effects department who devised an electro-magnetic device powered by a 12-volt car battery. Recently, in Australia, the professional company went to an adult "marital aid" store where they purchased an electric thrusting device which gave satisfaction – not for the first time, I gather. A more crude and reliable way of doing it might be to have a hole through the back of the dummy which should be flush with the scenery and to put a walking stick sized instrument through to the front of the said dummy and to make the appropriate movements as if the teeth are down the shorts. In Australia the noise was produced by hand-held castanets sometimes found in a variety drummers kit and which should be available at any large musical store.

ACT I

The set is an adaptation of the television set: two lifts upstage; about half a dozen steps lead down from the lifts to the main store. The Gentlemens' counter, left, has a pad and pencil, chalk and a phone on it. The Ladies' counter, right, has a signing-in book, pen and tape measure on it. Underneath the counter top is a drawer with a display model of underwear in it. At least three display dummies are in evidence. One female in short fur-trimmed nightdress, one female in top, skirt and loose-fitting knickers and one male with woollen bathing shorts. There are entrances to fitting rooms downstage left and downstage right. There are entrances upstage left and upstage right at the level of the bottom of the stairs.

MASH enters with a bucket and cloth and a vacuum cleaner, singing the first verse of "IF YOU WERE THE ONLY GIRL". He goes to the girl model which is covered with the flimsy nightdress with a fur hem. He starts to wash the model from the knees. He lifts the hem of the nightdress up and washes the model's bottom.

MR RUMBOLD *enters.*

RUMBOLD Good morning, Mash.

MASH Good morning, Rumbold.

RUMBOLD *Mister* Rumbold.

MASH Sorry, sir. I forgot I was just one of the lowly humble workers. *(He starts to wash the upper half of the model)*

RUMBOLD What are you doing, Mr Mash?

MASH Just cleaning up the models for the Common Market sales week. This is the French bridal nightie. Note the fur muff round the knees to keep the bride's ears warm during the honeymoon.

RUMBOLD Do you have to do that now?

MASH Oh, yes. Mrs Slocombe said they wanted titivating. *(He washes the model's bust)*

RUMBOLD You don't have to use a dirty old wet rag. Surely a feather duster would have the same effect?

MASH Last time I put a feather duster up a nightie it had a remarkable effect—I've still got the scars.

MISS BRAHMS enters from the lift, left. She has a suitcase and a large pregnant-looking bulge under her coat.

MISS BRAHMS Morning, Mr Rumbold.

RUMBOLD Good morning, Miss Brahms.

MISS BRAHMS Blimey—it nearly killed me carrying this load.

MASH Congratulations, darling, how long have you been in the club?

MISS BRAHMS Since this morning—it's the only way I could get a seat on the train. *(She opens her coat and pulls out a duffle bag)*

MASH goes to sponge down the next model.

RUMBOLD Mr Mash, do not do that in front of Miss Brahms.

MASH Sorry, sir. Can I give her a going over with the Goblin? *(He indicates the vacuum cleaner)* I'm talking about the model.

RUMBOLD Oh—all right—get on with it.

Turning on the vacuum cleaner, MASH goes to a model in skirt and blouse.

MASH *(to* MISS BRAHMS*)* Close your eyes, darling. *(To the model)* Hold your breath. *(He vacuums under the skirt. He pulls the vacuum pipe away and a pair of knickers are attached)* Blimey, look at that.

MISS BRAHMS Oh Mr Mash, you are disgusting.

MASH What are you going on about? I bet it's not the first time you've lost your knickers in a tube.

MASH *exits.*

MR LUCAS *enters from the lift left, on crutches, with a false plaster cast on his leg.*

LUCAS Morning all.

MISS BRAHMS Good heavens, what you been doing?

LUCAS *(taking off the plaster cast which is wrapped round a Wellington boot)* Nothing—this is the only way I can get a seat on the train with all them pregnant women about.

MISS BRAHMS Where's your suitcase?

LUCAS I left it at home.

MISS BRAHMS You silly berk. You know we're going straight from here to the airport when we close.

LUCAS *(moving to the book on the Ladies' counter to sign in)* It was too heavy for me to carry. My mum's taking it for me in her invalid car.

MISS BRAHMS Hope it's a bit warmer on the Costa Blanca than it is here.

LUCAS Just think of it, Shirley. You and me under the Spanish stars dancing cheek to cheek.

MISS BRAHMS With all the rest of the Department watching, you'll have to behave yourself.

LUCAS That won't be easy—the sight of you in your bikini will drive me wild with desire.

MISS BRAHMS I'll shove you in the pool to cool you off.

LUCAS Do you think they'll have a pool?

MISS BRAHMS Well, it said so in the brochure.

LUCAS I'll be able to tickle you in the deep end... *(He tickles her)*

MISS BRAHMS Get off.

LUCAS With your figure you won't need water wings.

MISS BRAHMS Pity you haven't got bigger earholes.

LUCAS Why?

MISS BRAHMS You could get a toothbrush in and clean your mind out.

The lift left opens. **MR GRAINGER** *steps out.*

LUCAS
MISS BRAHMS } *(together)* Morning, Mr Grainger.

GRAINGER Good morning. I wonder if you could help me. I have my old bag in the lift.

LUCAS Ah, did you persuade Mrs Grainger to come as well?

GRAINGER Just because we are going on holiday together you're not entitled to be facetious, Mr Lucas. *(He burps)* These travel pills are not agreeing with me at all.

MISS BRAHMS They're supposed to be for the plane, not the bus.

GRAINGER I know that, Miss Brahms. I thought I'd better try them out in case I needed pills to get over the travel pills.

LUCAS What happened to Captain Peacock this morning?

GRAINGER I saw him in the Sports Department purchasing some new balls.

LUCAS He's determined to enjoy his holiday, isn't he?

The lift door left opens to reveal **CAPTAIN PEACOCK.**

ALL Good morning, Captain Peacock.

PEACOCK *steps out of the lift with two suitcases.* MASH *is behind him, carrying a set of golf clubs.*

PEACOCK Ah, I see you're all ahead of me.

MASH *sticks the golf clubs between* PEACOCK*'s legs*

Good mo-o-o-r-n-i-ng.

MASH Sorry, Captain Peacock. I nearly got a hole-in-one there. Where would you like them?

PEACOCK Behind the counter, Mr Mash.

MASH I'm sorry I'm not coming with you in a way.

PEACOCK Yes, I understand the Grace Brothers' holiday deal was not available to manual and unskilled labour.

MASH Oh no, it wasn't that. I'm booked for the Seashells. Royalty goes there. I've been to all them Spanish places; a bit common if you ask me.

MASH *exits.*

PEACOCK *takes off his coat.*

PEACOCK And Mr Lucas, I hope I'm not going to see you standing around with your hands in your pockets again today.

LUCAS Certainly not, sir. I've sewn them up like you said. *(He demonstrates that all his pockets are sewn up)*

PEACOCK And straighten your tie, Mr Lucas.

LUCAS Oh, sorry, sir. *(He straightens his tie)*

PEACOCK *points to three pencils in* LUCAS*'s breast pocket.*

PEACOCK One pencil is sufficient.

LUCAS Yes, Captain Peacock. Shall I keep the HB or the extra soft?

PEACOCK If you had troubled to read the memo from the Accounts Department, you would see that they prefer ballpoints. Right, Mr Lucas.

LUCAS Ballpoints, Captain Peacock. *(He sees something on* **PEACOCK***'s collar)*

PEACOCK Any questions.

LUCAS Yes, sir. What's small, green and furry, with six legs?

PEACOCK Why do you ask, Mr Lucas?

LUCAS Because whatever it is, has just crept out of your carnation and crouched on your collar.

PEACOCK Deal with it, Mr Lucas.

LUCAS Certainly, sir. *(He puts his thumb on* **PEACOCK***'s collar and squashes the bug)* There, it's dead. Will there be anything else, sir?

PEACOCK Yes, get me a fifteen and a half collar from stock.

There is much banging upon the door of the lift right. This lift is never seen in the normal condition.

What on earth?

MRS SLOCOMBE *(in the lift)* Drat this thing. The damned door's stuck again.

MISS BRAHMS It's Mrs Slocombe, she's stuck in the lift.

LUCAS *and* **MISS BRAHMS** *go up the stairs and press buttons, etc. The door on the lift right opens to show that the lift has stuck about three feet above the level of the floor.* **MRS SLOCOMBE** *has to bend or kneel to be seen.*

MRS SLOCOMBE It's time somebody saw to this dratted thing.

LUCAS Come on—we'll help you.

MISS BRAHMS Pass your things out.

PEACOCK Take Mrs Slocombe's cases.

MRS SLOCOMBE How am I going to get down?

MISS BRAHMS Well, you'll have to back out.

MRS SLOCOMBE Would you mind holding my pussy? *(She hands out a cat basket)*

PEACOCK Mrs Slocombe, you're not taking that to Spain with you.

MRS SLOCOMBE Of course not. I'm dropping it into the pet department to look after till I'm back. Oh, dear, I hope I haven't forgotten my passport. *(She backs out, showing Union Jack knickers)*

LUCAS Don't worry—if you show the Spanish customs what you're showing us, I'm sure they'll know you're British.

MRS SLOCOMBE Captain Peacock, will you make Mr Lucas avert his gaze?

PEACOCK I'll come and help you myself.

MRS SLOCOMBE What makes you think that'll be any better? I bought these for the Common Market week.

LUCAS Let's hope there's no national disaster, otherwise you'll have to wear them at half mast.

MRS SLOCOMBE Couldn't I have a ladder?

LUCAS You've already got one. It goes very nearly out of sight.

MRS SLOCOMBE I'll bat you in the earhole when I get down.

MISS BRAHMS *brings a chair.*

MISS BRAHMS Here you are, Mrs Slocombe.

MRS SLOCOMBE Thank you, Miss Brahms. At least somebody's a Lady. Now I want you all to look the other way before I start again. *(She starts to climb down)*

MR MASH *enters with a feather duster, singing* **"UNDERNEATH THE ARCHES".** *He dusts* **MRS SLOCOMBE**'s *backside.*

Oooh...

MASH *(reciting)* I like to spread some happiness
Everywhere I pass,
That's why I took a bit of fluff,
Off Mrs Slocombe's...

PEACOCK Mr Mash...

MASH *exits.*

MRS SLOCOMBE That man. Ooh, what a humiliating experience.

LUCAS I think it's upset your pussy—it's miaowing.

PEACOCK Get behind your counter, Mr Lucas. The store will be open in a few minutes.

MRS SLOCOMBE *takes off her coat.* MR GRAINGER *is about to leave.*

Where are you going, Mr Grainger?

GRAINGER I'm afraid the thought of flying has brought on a touch of my old gastric trouble, Captain Peacock, so with your permission, I'm off to the little boys' room.

PEACOCK You have my permission.

LUCAS It's just as well.

GRAINGER By the way, they will have one in the aeroplane, won't they?

LUCAS If they don't, Mr Grainger, we'll tell the driver to stop just for you.

GRAINGER Can they do that—you know—I've often—oh, damn.

GRAINGER *hurries off.*

PEACOCK It has all the makings of an interesting flight. *(He looks at the book)* Mrs Slocombe, I see you haven't signed the book.

MRS SLOCOMBE All this red tape. I should have thought a sales assistant with my seniority would be past that sort of thing.

LUCAS Quite right, Mrs Slocombe. I mean, let's face it, you're past most sorts of thing.

MRS SLOCOMBE Can you hear me clearly, Mr Lucas?

LUCAS Yes, Mrs Slocombe.

MRS SLOCOMBE Well, would you mind shutting your cakehole. *(To* **PEACOCK***)* The juniors these days are very poor quality, are they not?

PEACOCK They are, Mrs Slocombe.

MRS SLOCOMBE Is it true that Mrs Peacock won't be accompanying us on our vacation?

PEACOCK Sadly no.

MRS SLOCOMBE We shall have to watch it, won't we?

PEACOCK Watch what, Mrs Slocombe?

MRS SLOCOMBE Well—you know—two unattached persons thrown together on a foreign shore—hot tropical nights, pulsating music—a couple of rum and cokes and who knows what can happen.

PEACOCK Don't worry, Mrs Slocombe, you may rely on me to behave like a gentleman.

MRS SLOCOMBE Yes, I thought so. *(She looks at the book)* Oh, I can hardly see to write my name.

MISS BRAHMS Get plastered again last night, did you?

MRS SLOCOMBE Certainly not, we just had a few gin and tonics. Well, one of the tonics must have been bad. They are sometimes, you know, because I came over all dizzy and Mrs Axelby had to put me to bed.

MISS BRAHMS Not with Mr Axelby.

MRS SLOCOMBE Certainly not, Miss Brahms.

PEACOCK *(after glancing round conspiratorily)* Talking of pubs reminds me of a bit of doggerel I picked up the mess.

MISS BRAHMS Really? What's that?

PEACOCK On the chest of a barmaid from Sale
Was tattoo'd all the prices of ale
Whilst upon her behind
For the sake of the blind
Was precisely the same, but in braille.

MRS SLOCOMBE *(po-faced)* Will that be all, Captain Peacock?

MISS BRAHMS *giggles.*

PEACOCK For the moment, Mrs Slocombe.

PEACOCK *moves away.*

MRS SLOCOMBE Oh, he's so coarse sometimes.

MISS BRAHMS If you think he's coarse, just wait till you get to Spain. Last time I was there I couldn't walk on the beach without having my bottom pinched.

MRS SLOCOMBE Really? Which particular beach was that?

MISS BRAHMS Any beach. As soon as they see a female bottom they go mad.

MRS SLOCOMBE It's just as well I've been slimming. At least they won't have such a big target. Let's see what I've got it down to. *(She picks up a tape measure and puts it round herself)* What does it read?

MISS BRAHMS Oh, doesn't it seem a lot in metric.

MRS SLOCOMBE Why, what does it say?

MISS BRAHMS Fifty-four whatever-they-ares.

MRS SLOCOMBE Centipedes, Miss Brahms.

MISS BRAHMS Well, whatever they are, you've put on two more.

MRS SLOCOMBE I don't know how you stay so slim. You must be starving yourself.

MISS BRAHMS Well, I have a big meal every night.

MRS SLOCOMBE I don't know how you can afford it.

MISS BRAHMS Well, I can't—I have to keep going out with men I don't like, just to keep body and soul together.

MRS SLOCOMBE Oh—I couldn't do that.

MISS BRAHMS It's easy. I wear my low-cut dress—they have a good look, and I have a good nosh.

MRS SLOCOMBE But these days they expect something afterwards, don't they?

MISS BRAHMS Oh, yes, but they don't get it.

MRS SLOCOMBE But why do they keep asking you out?

MISS BRAHMS It's the same principle as a fruit machine. Once they've invested, they go on and on hoping to hit the jackpot...

MRS SLOCOMBE They'd have to pull the handle a lot of times to get my cherries up.

MISS BRAHMS Here—you didn't forget your passport, did you?

MRS SLOCOMBE No, I had a new photo took. Look.

MISS BRAHMS Oh, isn't it awful.

Another picture falls out of MRS SLOCOMBE'*s passport.*

'Ere, what's this?

MRS SLOCOMBE That's one I had took on the front at Yarmouth.

MISS BRAHMS Don't your figure look smashing?

MRS SLOCOMBE It's not mine. It's Raquel Welch's. It was one of those where you stick your head through the hole. I sent it to the lonely hearts magazine and I couldn't open the door for letters.

The store bell rings.

PEACOCK *begins to change his collar.*

PEACOCK Places everyone.

MASH *enters with a very large crate.*

MASH Tote that barge, lift that bale. C. O. D. from British Rail.

PEACOCK Mr Mash, how many times have I told you that goods must not be delivered on the floor after the store is open.

MASH It's a special, Captain. Marked most urgent.

RUMBOLD *enters.*

PEACOCK If Mr Rumbold sees it, his eyes will pop out of his head.

RUMBOLD I've just heard that a package has been delivered on the floor.

LUCAS Look, his ears have popped out of his head.

PEACOCK I have just castigated Mr Mash.

LUCAS Does that mean he can sing in the choir now?

RUMBOLD Open the case and get it out of the way at once.

MASH *starts to open the crate.*

This whole department is getting very slack, Captain Peacock. We expect you to get dressed before you arrive at Grace Brothers—I do not expect to find you unattired at five past nine.

PEACOCK *(fixing his collar)* I can explain, sir.

RUMBOLD I don't want to hear any excuses. I want a word with the members of your department. Where's Mr Humphries?

MR HUMPHRIES, *carrying a handbag, pops out of the crate* **MASH** *delivered.*

HUMPHRIES I'm free. Oh, give me a hand somebody—they dropped me at Euston.

PEACOCK Mr Humphries. I trust you can explain arriving like a Jack-in-the-Box at five past nine.

HUMPHRIES Well, it was like this. I've got this friend, you see, who's very possessive, who waited all night outside my flat to say goodbye. Well, I didn't want a big emotional scene, you see—

LUCAS Couldn't you have got the police to remove him?

HUMPHRIES What makes you think it was a him? Anyway, I phoned British Rail and they sent these two big men who stuffed me in the box.

MRS SLOCOMBE Oh, wasn't it claustrophobic?

HUMPHRIES Well, yes, it was until the big one got out.

LUCAS Lucky you didn't crush your handbag.

HUMPHRIES It is not my handbag. I mean, am I the sort of person who'd carry a crocodile handbag with suede shoes? I'm having it repaired for a friend.

MRS SLOCOMBE She must be rich to afford a crocodile handbag.

HUMPHRIES What makes you think it's a she?

GRAINGER *enters.*

RUMBOLD Never mind, settle down. Where's Grainger?

GRAINGER *(coming in)* Sorry, Mr Rumbold, I took a couple of travel pills this morning and—oh damn...

GRAINGER *goes out again.*

HUMPHRIES They're certainly making him travel.

RUMBOLD Captain Peacock, I want to have a word with the staff while the store is quiet.

PEACOCK Certainly, sir. Mrs Slocombe, are you free?

MRS SLOCOMBE As soon as I've put up my underwear, Captain Peacock. *(She opens a drawer at waist height and takes out underwear display and puts it on the counter. She tries to shut the drawer. It sticks)* Oh, drat it. *(She turns and bangs it shut with her backside)*

PEACOCK Miss Brahms, are you free?

MISS BRAHMS Coming, Captain Peacock.

PEACOCK Mr Lucas, are you free?

LUCAS *(looking round)* Yes, I think I'm just about free.

PEACOCK Are you free, Mr Humphries?

HUMPHRIES I've never been free, Captain Peacock, but I am available.

> **GRAINGER** *enters.*

PEACOCK Are you free, Mr Grainger?

GRAINGER Yes, it was a false alarm.

MASH I'm free an' all.

PEACOCK But you are not required, Mr Mash.

MASH Oh, it's like that, is it? Come the revolution we'll all be equal and then *I'll* be driving round in a big car.

RUMBOLD Mr Mash, I wonder if you'd be kind enough to start bringing up those German goods.

MASH Yah, herr jugen. Earen.

RUMBOLD Do not refer to me in that way.

LUCAS No, leave out the hair.

PEACOCK Pay attention, please. Mr Rumbold has something to say.

RUMBOLD Now, as you know, the wind of change is blowing through Grace Brothers.

GRAINGER Oh, damn.

GRAINGER *exits.*

PEACOCK *(calling after him)* We'll keep you informed, Mr Grainger.

RUMBOLD Now, while we're all away on our holiday at the Don Bernardo Hotel, the store is being redecorated. On our return we shall be having a series of campaigns to push goods from the Common Market, commencing with Germany.

MRS SLOCOMBE I don't see why we should push jerry goods, we have enough trouble selling our own.

RUMBOLD Do I detect an anti-German feeling?

MRS SLOCOMBE You do, Mr Rumbold. Some of us haven't forgotten the war. I remember being flung flat on my back on Clapham Common by a landmine. And the German air force was responsible.

LUCAS All the other times she was flat on her back the American air force was responsible.

MRS SLOCOMBE Would you please knock it off.

LUCAS She even remembers what she said.

RUMBOLD Look, don't let us go into all this. I know how excited we're all getting at the prospect of starting our holiday this very day, but—

PEACOCK *(interrupting)* Mr Rumbold, speaking for myself, I don't think we should over-emphasise the excitement of going away "en masse" as it were.

MRS SLOCOMBE I'm not a bit excited about going away with him.

PEACOCK I had personally planned a nostalgic visit to Mersa Matrah with Mrs Peacock to visit once again the scene of our great assault.

MISS BRAHMS Was that your honeymoon?

PEACOCK I was referring to the Eighth Army.

RUMBOLD Were you in it?

PEACOCK No—I was just referring to it.

MRS SLOCOMBE My friend's very disappointed. We were both going to Olympia to show our pussies.

HUMPHRIES My friend's very disappointed as well.

LUCAS Why? Were you going to Olympia too?

HUMPHRIES No, we were going camping.

RUMBOLD Well, you all had the opportunity to make your own arrangements and let's face it, if it wasn't for the generosity of young Mr Grace, where else could you get a week in Spain for twenty pounds at a one-star hotel?

MRS SLOCOMBE I've been wondering about that—how good is a one-star hotel?

PEACOCK Let's put it this way, Mrs Slocombe, there is no such thing as a nostar hotel.

RUMBOLD This is all beside the point.

GRAINGER *enters.*

GRAINGER Have I missed anything?

HUMPHRIES Not unless you were going to Olympia.

RUMBOLD What I am trying to say is this. Before we go, young Mr Grace is most anxious for us to check the German goods and our methods of displaying them, so we can get a good start as soon as we come back.

MRS SLOCOMBE I hope he's not still keen on us wearing them German costumes and doing that daft dance.

RUMBOLD It was all agreed at the meeting, Mrs Slocombe, and after all, we have rehearsed it.

HUMPHRIES You're telling me. Last night my back was so bad, my friend had to give me a going over with brown paper and a hot iron.

LUCAS We didn't rehearse last night.

HUMPHRIES I know, but I wasn't going to tell, was I?

MRS SLOCOMBE Well, I'm against the whole idea. I don't like the Germans. They've got no sense of humour.

LUCAS Well, won't there be a lot of jerries in Spain?

HUMPHRIES *(looking at* **GRAINGER***)* I sincerely hope so.

RUMBOLD Right, that's settled then.

NURSE enters with an enormous syringe behind her back.

Ah, Matron, I see you're ready to give the injections.

MRS SLOCOMBE Injections? What injections?

RUMBOLD Grace Brothers does not want you to take any risk, so we're giving you free immunization against cholera. You go first, Mrs Slocombe.

MRS SLOCOMBE But the mere sight of a needle makes me pass out. I can't even knit.

MISS BRAHMS The last time I had it in the arm it left a nasty mark.

RUMBOLD You won't have to have it in the arm.

HUMPHRIES I'll go first.

The **NURSE** *produces the enormous syringe.*

You go first.

MISS BRAHMS Come on, let's get it over with. *(She takes* **MRS SLOCOMBE** *by the hand)*

MRS SLOCOMBE These holiday pamphlets are all alike. All they show you is sun, sea and sex—but they never talk about a jacksy full of vaccine.

MRS SLOCOMBE exits with MISS BRAHMS and the NURSE.

PEACOCK In Mrs Slocombe's absence, shall I put Mr Humphries in Ladies underwear?

HUMPHRIES You wait till you're asked.

RUMBOLD Yes, Captain Peacock, do that.

PEACOCK Take over, Mr Humphries.

*A **LADY CUSTOMER** enters. She has an ample bosom.*

HUMPHRIES Are you being served, madam?

LADY Well, I was looking for somebody of the same sex.

HUMPHRIES Aren't we all.

LADY Oh, well, er, you see this suit I'm wearing, I'm not very happy with it.

HUMPHRIES No, I quite understand, madam. It is a bit old-fashioned. You want something new.

LADY It is new, I bought it here yesterday.

HUMPHRIES Did you? Let me have a look at it again. Oh yes, of course, one of our revival lines. An echo of the forties.

LADY I'm not happy with the fit—it's a bit large.

HUMPHRIES Yes, some of the revived lines are a bit loose. Let's have a look at the size. Oh, yes, it's a revived forty-five.

LADY I'd like a size smaller.

HUMPHRIES I regret, madam, as you've worn it, we can't do that—but we can soon alter it. Now, how is it under the arms? Put them out, will you.

*The **LADY** puts her arms out. **HUMPHRIES** puts his hands under her arms.*

Now down, please.

*The **LADY** does so, trapping his hands.*

Oh, that is cosy. I mean that's a cosy fit. If I could just have them back.

She releases his hands.

Now, how's the chest?

LADY I'm not complaining about the chest.

HUMPHRIES No, I don't wonder.

LADY It's the skirt.

HUMPHRIES I'll get my chalk. *(He goes to his counter to get his chalk)*

LUCAS You'll need a bigger piece than that.

HUMPHRIES *(returning)* Now which part of the skirt, madam?

LADY *(embarrassed)* Well, er, it's what one might call the derrière.

HUMPHRIES I specialise in derrières. Now what precisely is the trouble?

LADY Well, it seems to droop a bit.

HUMPHRIES What? The derrière or the skirt?

LADY The skirt seems to droop at the back.

HUMPHRIES Ah, yes, it wants taking in a bit here. Would madam brace herself for a quick tickle. *(He chalks on the backside)*

LADY Ooooh.

He chalks again.

Ooooh.

HUMPHRIES That didn't hurt, did it?

LADY No, I rather liked it.

HUMPHRIES Yes, it is nice, isn't it.

LADY But if you take it in there, it'll ride up when I sit down.

HUMPHRIES Quite right, madam. *(He grabs the end of his sleeve with his hand and busily rubs out the chalk mark)* No tucks in the derrière.

*The **LADY** giggles.*

LADY It's the waist, you see. Look, you can get your hand in.

HUMPHRIES Does madam regard that as a disadvantage?

LADY Yes, look.

> **HUMPHRIES** *does so.*

HUMPHRIES Oh, the things you see when you haven't got your gun. *(He pulls the back of the waist to test the waist band)* Oh dear, I've dropped me chalk down there. Don't move. *(He pulls the waistband back and peers down)*

LADY Can you see?

HUMPHRIES You haven't got a torch, have you? Tell you what, jump up and down and see if anything pops out.

> *She jumps up and down with obvious effect on her ample bosom.*

Stop! I think something's going to pop out. Hang on, I've spotted it. *(He takes the metal end of his tape measure and bends it into a hook)* It's just like *Jaws*, isn't it? *(He dangles the hook down the skirt)*

LADY How are you getting on?

HUMPHRIES Don't breathe—I think it's taken the bait. *(He pulls. The end is stuck)* Oh, heck, it's stuck in the gusset. Ah, I can see it. I tell you what's going to happen. You shut your eyes, think of England and I'll make a quick grab. *(He does so)* High up. *(He grabs and retrieves the chalk)*

LADY I didn't feel a thing.

HUMPHRIES Neither did I.

LADY Oh, you are clever.

HUMPHRIES Not all that clever, I've lost me watch.

> *The* **LADY** *starts to retrieve it.*

> **PEACOCK** *enters.*

PEACOCK What on earth is happening, Mr Humphries?

HUMPHRIES The Lady's trying to get hold of my Rolex.

PEACOCK Your what?

HUMPHRIES My Rolex watch. It's a good job it's shock-proof.

The LADY *produces the watch.*

PEACOCK Our Lady assistants will attend to you if you'd care to wait a few moments. They're just having smallpox and cholera at the moment.

LADY I'll come back when they're better.

The LADY *exits.*

MRS SLOCOMBE *and* MISS BRAHMS *enter, in step, holding their backsides.*

MR HUMPHRIES *starts to sing the* **"SAND DANCE"** *(Snake Charmer in Old Baghdad).*

HUMPHRIES Here's Wilson and Keppel—where's Betty?

MRS SLOCOMBE By gum, my bum's numb.

MISS BRAHMS I'd rather have had cholera.

The NURSE *enters.*

NURSE I'm ready for the gentlemen now.

PEACOCK We'd better leave somebody in the Department. Would you mind staying behind, Mr Grainger, and taking charge of the floor?

GRAINGER With great pleasure, Captain Peacock.

LUCAS Ah, well...here we go.

LUCAS *exits.*

HUMPHRIES It's a far, far better thing I do.

HUMPHRIES *exits.*

PEACOCK Do I take it, nurse, that we have to remove our trousers in front of you?

NURSE Yes—but don't worry, I don't look.

PEACOCK That gives me a lot of confidence.

PEACOCK *exits.*

During the following, while they are off stage, **PEACOCK,** **HUMPHRIES** *and* **LUCAS** *dress in the German costume.*

The lift bell dings and a **MALE CUSTOMER** *enters.*

GRAINGER Can I help you, sir?

MALE CUSTOMER I'd like a pair of gloves, please.

GRAINGER Certainly, sir. Oh, damn, are you free, Mrs Slocombe?

MRS SLOCOMBE Yes, I'm free, Mr Grainger.

GRAINGER Would you take a pair of gloves. I have an urgent call.

GRAINGER *exits.*

MRS SLOCOMBE What sort of gloves does sir require, sir?

MALE CUSTOMER Fur.

MRS SLOCOMBE *takes a pair of gloves off display.*

MRS SLOCOMBE These gloves are very popular. They're rabbit.

MALE CUSTOMER Are they real rabbit?

MRS SLOCOMBE Oh—guaranteed.

MISS BRAHMS Yes—we daren't leave two pairs in the same drawer together.

MRS SLOCOMBE Thank you, Miss Brahms.

MALE CUSTOMER I have rather big hands.

MRS SLOCOMBE These are the largest size.

MALE CUSTOMER In that case, they'll do beautifully.

MRS SLOCOMBE Cash or account?

MALE CUSTOMER Account.

MRS SLOCOMBE I'll just make the bill out.

MALE CUSTOMER I haven't finished yet.

MRS SLOCOMBE Oh, was there something else?

MALE CUSTOMER What have you got in Y-fronts?

MRS SLOCOMBE Y-fronts? I'm not too familiar with the stock. Miss Brahms— *(She indicates the drawers)* Come and have a look into the gentlemen's drawers.

The CUSTOMER *starts to take off his trousers.*

Not yours, sir. I was referring to these here departmental drawers.

MISS BRAHMS Here we are, underwear. Would these be the ones? Jokey shorts.

MRS SLOCOMBE Jockey shorts, Miss Brahms.

MISS BRAHMS Do jockeys have to have special underwear, then?

MRS SLOCOMBE As you see, we're rather out of our area here. *(She whispers)* What size do you think he wants?

MISS BRAHMS Well, he's got big hands.

MRS SLOCOMBE What's that got to do with it?

MISS BRAHMS Well, you know the saying "Big hands, big..."

MRS SLOCOMBE I'm quite sure that's got nothing to do with it. But judging by the size of his nose, we'll give him large. There we are, sir, will there be anything else?

MALE CUSTOMER Yes, I want a pair of trousers.

MRS SLOCOMBE I see. Well, could you come back later?

MALE CUSTOMER No, I'm in a hurry.

MRS SLOCOMBE Do you know your size?

MALE CUSTOMER No. You'll have to measure me.

MRS SLOCOMBE Tape measure, Miss Brahms.

　　MISS BRAHMS *hands one off the counter.*

　　Get a pad and pencil to take this down.

　　MISS BRAHMS *goes to the other end of the counter.*

　　Excuse me, sir. *(She puts the tape round his hips)* Will you be having that bulge there, sir?

MALE CUSTOMER Yes—that's my spectacle case. *(He shows the spectacle case from his hip pocket)*

MRS SLOCOMBE I see. Are you ready, Miss Brahms?

MISS BRAHMS Yes—I'm ready.

MRS SLOCOMBE Thirty-eight, including the spectacles.

MISS BRAHMS Including the what?

MRS SLOCOMBE Spectacles, Miss Brahms. Does sir happen to know his inside leg?

MALE CUSTOMER No, you'll have to take it.

MRS SLOCOMBE We'll have to take it, Miss Brahms.

MISS BRAHMS Couldn't we give him an estimate?

MRS SLOCOMBE No, take it, Miss Brahms.

MISS BRAHMS I'm not going to take it.

MRS SLOCOMBE Why not?

MISS BRAHMS I'm frightened.

MRS SLOCOMBE What of?

MISS BRAHMS The unknown.

MRS SLOCOMBE Never mind—I've got an idea. Hold the tape like this.

She gets **MISS BRAHMS** *to dangle the tape with the end at floor level. She gets an umbrella.*

Was sir by any chance in the army?

MALE CUSTOMER Yes, I was.

MRS SLOCOMBE Good... About turn.

He faces away from her. **MISS BRAHMS** *stands in front of him with the tape.*

Stand at ease.

He does so. She whips the umbrella between his legs. As the end stops up against the tape, **MISS BRAHMS** *calls out.*

MISS BRAHMS Thirty-one.

MRS SLOCOMBE What colour, sir?

MALE CUSTOMER *(falsetto)* Fawn.

GRAINGER *enters.*

MRS SLOCOMBE Sale, Mr Grainger. Thirty-four—thirty-one trousers in fawn.

GRAINGER Thank you, Mrs Slocombe.

MRS SLOCOMBE *(seeing* **PEACOCK** *and* **HUMPHRIES** *approaching)* Ay up—here comes the walking wounded.

HUMPHRIES *enters, holding his backside.*

HUMPHRIES My leg won't bend at the knee. I hope it's not permanent, I used to have such a pretty walk.

MRS SLOCOMBE What happened to the gallant Captain Peacock?

HUMPHRIES He didn't take it so well.

PEACOCK *enters, limping badly.*

PEACOCK I wouldn't have gone if I'd know she was going to throw the needle like a dart.

HUMPHRIES Think yourself lucky she didn't get a bullseye.

MRS SLOCOMBE Would you like to sit down, Captain Peacock?

PEACOCK I don't think so.

HUMPHRIES Speaking for myself, I shall be strap-hanging all the way to Barcelona.

MRS SLOCOMBE Never mind. The pain wears off after about five minutes.

PEACOCK I'm unspeakably glad to hear it.

MRS SLOCOMBE Then you get dizzy. *(She crosses confidentially to* **CAPTAIN PEACOCK***)* I've got a flask of brandy in my first-aid cabinet, in the fitting room—just for emergencies, you know. Would you care to join me?

PEACOCK Thank you, Mrs Slocombe. I shall be honoured.

They go towards the door, arm in arm.

MRS SLOCOMBE Miss Brahms, take over while Captain Peacock and I have a quick one in the fitting room.

MRS SLOCOMBE *and* **PEACOCK** *exit.*

MISS BRAHMS Blimey, what was in their injections?

LUCAS *enters.*

HUMPHRIES Where have you been?

LUCAS I stopped off to chat up that blonde in the joke department.

HUMPHRIES You've been told off for that sort of thing before.

LUCAS I know. The supervisor saw me, so I had to pretend I was a customer and buy these. *(He places a pair of clockwork false teeth on the counter and they chatter up and down)*

HUMPHRIES Look out, here comes Big Ears.

LUCAS *picks the teeth up and tries to put them in his pocket, but realizes they are sewn up, puts his hands behind his back.*

RUMBOLD *enters and approaches him.*

RUMBOLD Ah, Mr Lucas.

LUCAS *backs towards a dummy left. It is a full-length male dummy wearing wool bathing shorts*

LUCAS Yes, Mr Rumbold?

RUMBOLD Where is Captain Peacock?

LUCAS He's just gone in there, sir. *(He starts to indicate with his hand, but realizing that it holds the teeth, he indicates with the other hand)*

RUMBOLD What have you got behind your back?

LUCAS Nothing, sir.

RUMBOLD Have you been smoking on the floor?

LUCAS No, sir, I never smoke on the floor.

RUMBOLD You've got something in your hand.

LUCAS No, sir, look. *(He shows him one hand)*

RUMBOLD What about the other one?

LUCAS *changes the teeth and shows the other hand.*

Both, Mr Lucas.

LUCAS Both, sir?

RUMBOLD Both.

Unseen by RUMBOLD, LUCAS *appears to put the teeth down the front of the bathing trunks of the dummy. He then shows both hands.*

Thank you, Mr Lucas. You may go back to your counter.

LUCAS *does so.*

PEACOCK *and* **MRS SLOCOMBE** *enter. She carries a flask of brandy. She hides it when she sees* **RUMBOLD.**

Ah, Peacock, would you mind checking this list of German goods with me?

PEACOCK *crosses.*

PEACOCK Certainly, sir.

RUMBOLD And you, Mr Humphries.

They all go into a huddle. The teeth start to move inside the trunks. LUCAS *notices. He wonders if he dare retrieve them. He starts to walk towards them. The teeth stop.* LUCAS *stops.*

PEACOCK *(glancing up temporarily)* Your counter, Mr Lucas.

LUCAS Yes, Captain Peacock. *(He goes back to his counter)*

MISS BRAHMS *crosses left, carrying a package. The teeth start again.* **MISS BRAHMS** *stops dead. The teeth stop. She turns, crosses to* **MRS SLOCOMBE** *and whispers to her about it, miming the chatter with one hand.* **MRS SLOCOMBE** *looks. The teeth are still.* **MISS BRAHMS** *mimes again.* **MRS SLOCOMBE** *crosses. She stops. She puts her glasses on. The teeth start again, she jumps. She staggers back to the counter. She looks again. The teeth stop. She takes a swig of brandy.*

She decides to tell **CAPTAIN PEACOCK.** *She crosses to him and beckons him from the group. With her back to the audience, she whispers in his ear, miming the same way as* **MISS BRAHMS** *mimed.* **PEACOCK** *looks. The teeth are still.* **MRS SLOCOMBE** *mimes again.* **PEACOCK** *crosses, taking out his glasses. He puts them on and looks. The teeth are still. He takes his glasses off and is about to turn away. The teeth start again. He jumps. He returns* *to* **MRS SLOCOMBE.** *She offers the flask. He declines. She takes a swig.*

PEACOCK *crosses to* **HUMPHRIES. RUMBOLD** *goes to show* **MRS SLOCOMBE** *the list of figures.* **PEACOCK** *whispers to* **HUMPHRIES. HUMPHRIES** *faints at the thought.* **PEACOCK** *holds him and slaps his face to make him come round.* **PEACOCK** *puts his hand out to* **MRS SLOCOMBE** *without looking at her. Still talking to* **MR RUMBOLD,** *she puts the flask in* **PEACOCK**'*s hand.* **PEACOCK** *gives a swig to* **HUMPHRIES** *and hands it back.*

HUMPHRIES *revives and takes a couple of tentative steps towards the model. The teeth start again.* **HUMPHRIES** *goes back and grabs hold of* **PEACOCK**'*s hand. The teeth stop. They both approach hand in hand.* **HUMPHRIES** *stretches out a tentative hand. The teeth start again.* **HUMPHRIES** *jumps into* **PEACOCK**'*s arms.* **PEACOCK** *puts him down and goes for a heavy-handled walking stick. He is about to wallop the teeth.* **HUMPHRIES** *stops him with alarm. He mimes that he will get it out.* **HUMPHRIES** *goes to the dummy. He turns it away from* **PEACOCK** *and the audience. He puts his hand down the front.*

HUMPHRIES *(yelling)* It bit me! *(He brings out his hand with the teeth gripping his fingers)*

RUMBOLD   Please come over here and stop messing about, Captain Peacock. We must get our teeth into this German problem.

They rejoin him.

Well, you've seen the list of goods. These must be checked before we go on holiday.

Moans from the staff.

And there's one other thing. Young Mr Grace is most anxious to see the German dance that you'll be performing during the German sales week.

ALL Oh no.

MRS SLOCOMBE Well, speaking for myself, and I'm sure I'm unanimous in this, I feel right daft doing that German dance dressed like this.

MISS BRAHMS I think we should wait till we put on the proper costumes.

ALL Hear, hear.

RUMBOLD I do agree, Miss Brahms. Fortunately, the proper costumes have just arrived, so there's nothing to stand in our way.

MRS SLOCOMBE But people will see us.

RUMBOLD Notice has already gone up in the lift that this department is temporarily closed.

PEACOCK I trust if I join this charade I shall be given some garment which will be in keeping with my position.

LUCAS Why don't you dress up as Hitler?

RUMBOLD Don't worry, Captain Peacock, I shall see that whatever you wear gives you the appropriate air of authority.

MASH enters, wearing a Hindenberg helmet. He is pushing a trolley.

MASH Achtung, achtung. Get your kraut gear here.

RUMBOLD That will do, Mr Mash. *(To the others)* Sign for those goods and then go and get changed.

RUMBOLD *exits.*

MISS BRAHMS Would you believe it? They're making us work right up to the last second.

PEACOCK Well, I suppose it's the least we can do for Grace Brothers. After all, they are subsidising our holiday.

MASH Here you are, a couple of German signs. *(He holds up signs reading "einfahrt" and "ausfahrt")*

MRS SLOCOMBE *(reading)* Einfahrt. Ausfahrt.

GRAINGER *enters.*

GRAINGER Oh, damn...

GRAINGER *exits again.*

PEACOCK Einfahrt means "Way In". Ausfahrt means "Way Out".

MRS SLOCOMBE Descriptive language, isn't it?

MASH Four boxes of whatever they are.

MRS SLOCOMBE *takes a box and reads.*

MRS SLOCOMBE Sex underhosen. I wonder what's inside.

PEACOCK Don't get carried away, Mrs Slocombe. Underhosen literally translated means undertrousers.

MISS BRAHMS Undertrousers. Do you mean knickers?

MRS SLOCOMBE I'm not selling German sex knickers.

PEACOCK Sex, Mrs Slocombe, is the word they use for six in Germany.

MISS BRAHMS What do they use for sex?

MASH Same as they use in England.

PEACOCK Will you hurry up, Mr Mash.

MASH There you are, twelve bras.

MRS SLOCOMBE And what's German for that? *(She looks at the box)* Bustenhalter. Bustenhalter—doesn't it sound crude.

MISS BRAHMS Let's have a look.

They extract a large canvas bra.

Bustenhalter. It'd halt anything, that would—including a bus.

MRS SLOCOMBE Heavens above—what size is that?

MISS BRAHMS It says Klein.

PEACOCK Klein, Miss Brahms, means small.

MRS SLOCOMBE My—they're well built, those German girls, aren't they?

MASH *(handing a box to the men)* Here's yours.

LUCAS *(reading)* One dozen strumpfs. *(He takes them out)* Oh, look—they're socks.

HUMPHRIES If we're going to sell that lot, we'll have to pull our strumpfs up. *(He takes out a pair of long johns)* Oh look—long Johanns.

MR RUMBOLD *puts his head in.*

RUMBOLD Aren't you all changed yet?

PEACOCK Just checking the goods, sir.

RUMBOLD Well, hurry it up, Peacock. Young Mr Grace is waiting.

PEACOCK Right. Changing rooms, everybody.

RUMBOLD, PEACOCK, MISS BRAHMS *and* MRS SLOCOMBE *exit.*

The phone rings.

HUMPHRIES You'd better answer it, Mr Lucas.

LUCAS *(picking up the phone)* Menswear. *(He listens)* I see, sir. *(To* HUMPHRIES*)* There's a customer here can't come to be measured for a suit, so would like us to send one.

HUMPHRIES What size and colour?

LUCAS *(into the phone)* Can I have your size and colour, sir. *(He listens, then to* HUMPHRIES*)* He's white, but he doesn't know his size.

HUMPHRIES I'll take the phone. *(Into the phone)* Have you got a tape measure? ...Well, you measure yourself and we'll write it down... You can't have it for a fortnight, we're all going away on holiday—yes, all the men—yes, isn't it cosy.

(*To* LUCAS) He's got a nice voice. Are you ready? ...Now hold it between the thumb and forefinger of the left hand...the tape, and we'll do the chest first. Now swing it behind your back and run it through your left hand—keeping a firm grip with your left, bring the two ends round to the front, breathe in—now out. And keep your finger on the mark and tell me what it reads... You can't read it because you're not what, sir? (*To* LUCAS) He's not wearing his glasses... Oh, he's found them—but he had to let go of the tape to do it. (*Into the phone*) Well, let's start with something easy, like your arm—now put one end of the tape on the shoulder seam of your jacket... (*To* LUCAS) He's wearing a sweater. (*Into the phone*) Well, just put it on where your shoulder ends and your arm begins—right. (*To* LUCAS) I wish I hadn't started.

LUCAS   You're working well.

HUMPHRIES   Now, with one end on your shoulder, stretch out your arm to its fullest extent and tell me how long it is to your wrist... What's that? ...What, you're very faint—can you shout? (*He shouts*) Can you hear me—oh dear. (*To* LUCAS) He's got the phone in the hand of the arm we're trying to measure. Hallo, bring the phone back to your ear—that's better. Now, what does the tape read? ...Six inches... Oh dear, sir, just let your arm hang down by your side—and let the tape dangle down. Now what does it read? ...Good. (*To* LUCAS) We've got one—yes—forty-eight inches... I see, from your hand to the floor.

LUCAS   He must be standing like that. (*He puts hand on hip*)

HUMPHRIES   I said he had a nice voice. (*Into the phone*) We'll take that as an outside leg measurement... And while we're in that area, we'll do the inside leg. This should be fun.

GRAINGER *enters, wearing a German costume, lederhosen, etc.*

GRAINGER   I think this has gone far enough, Mr Humphries. I'll takeover now.

HUMPHRIES Hang on, sir. I'm passing you over to Rumpelstiltskin.

GRAINGER *takes the phone.*

GRAINGER Good morning, sir, Grainger the senior assistant here, what colour suit did you have in mind—dark blue. How tall are you, sir? ...Five ten.

LUCAS *makes a note of the measurements.*

Weight, sir? Eleven stone, four pounds. Thank you, sir, that's all we need. *(He hangs up)* As soon as we get back, send off a dark blue forty-two regular and when you get the cheque, credit the sale to me.

LUCAS Yes, Mr Grainger. What's the customer's address?

GRAINGER Oh, damn.

HUMPHRIES Aren't you going anywhere?

LUCAS *and* **HUMPHRIES** *exit.*

RUMBOLD *enters in lederhosen. He carries a squeeze-box.*

RUMBOLD Ah, I see you're ready, Mr Grainger. I hope you'll be with us long enough to demonstrate the dance.

GRAINGER So do I.

PEACOCK *enters, dressed in lederhosen.*

PEACOCK Mr Rumbold, I have a very serious complaint.

RUMBOLD Not the same one as Mr Grainger I hope.

PEACOCK You did assure me that my costume would give me the appropriate air of authority. Well, I'm getting a lot of air but very little authority.

RUMBOLD You have my permission to wear a bigger brush in your hat.

PEACOCK Thank you, Mr Rumbold.

MISS BRAHMS *enters, wearing very short shorts and braces.*

MISS BRAHMS How shall I wear my braces? Like this or like this? *(She puts them inside and outside and centre of her bust)*

PEACOCK You have a couple of problems there.

MISS BRAHMS Well, you're men, you wear braces, you should know.

PEACOCK We don't have the same sort of problem. Why don't you take 'em off altogether?

MISS BRAHMS If I did, my trousers would fall down.

RUMBOLD Never mind that, Miss Brahms. Where's Mrs Slocombe?

MISS BRAHMS Well, when she bent down to put her boots on, she came over all dizzy, so she had another quick brandy to revive herself. I think she's revived herself too much.

MRS SLOCOMBE *is heard singing, off, à la Marlene Dietrich "UNDERNEATH THE LAMPLIGHT".*

MRS SLOCOMBE *appears in costume, the same as the others. She has her braces crossed. She carries the flask.*

MRS SLOCOMBE *(taking a drink)* This hat's too tight, it's making me giddy. *(She sees the others)* Oh, blimey. *(She laughs)* You've no idea how stupid you look. *(She drains the flask)* It's very inoxuous, this brandy, isn't it?

PEACOCK You want to watch out—it creeps up on you.

RUMBOLD I think it's overtaken her.

MRS SLOCOMBE *(inspecting* **MISS BRAHMS***)* If you wear your braces like mine, Miss Brahms, it's much more feminine— you haven't been on the brandy, have you? You're waving about a lot—stand still.

MISS BRAHMS Blimey, half the Ladies Department is *hors de combat.*

MRS SLOCOMBE You watch your language, my girl.

LUCAS *enters, and whistles.*

HUMPHRIES *enters on tiptoe, wearing very tight lederhosen.*

HUMPHRIES I don't know why it is, but my eyes are watering.

MRS SLOCOMBE Somebody twiddle his knob, he's out of focus.

PEACOCK Places, everybody, ready for the dance.

MRS SLOCOMBE Oh, the dance. *(She slaps her knees and thighs and does a bit of the dance)*

HUMPHRIES Oh, stop her, someone, she'll do herself a mischief.

LUCAS You're right. If all that starts wobbling, we'll never stop it.

RUMBOLD *(looking at the lift indicator)* He's coming. Places everybody.

PEACOCK Places.

The lift doors open to reveal MR GRACE *being pushed in a wheelchair by the* NURSE.

MR GRACE Good morning, everybody.

ALL Good morning, Mr Grace.

GRAINGER How nice to see you, Mr Grace.

MR GRACE Good morning, sonny.

RUMBOLD We're ready with the dance, sir.

MRS SLOCOMBE *hears and starts to dance.*

PEACOCK Not yet, Mrs Slocombe.

MRS SLOCOMBE As long as you realize I've done half of it already.

RUMBOLD Right, I shall give you the usual introduction. *(He plays his squeeze box)*

They dance 48 bars of a Bavarian thigh-slapping, hand-clapping dance, linking arms, changing partners. This includes pretend face slapping in time with the music and hand claps. During the dance, MRS SLOCOMBE *slaps* CAPTAIN PEACOCK'*s face rather hard. He retaliates.*

MRS SLOCOMBE You're not supposed to do it like that—you're supposed to be gentle.

PEACOCK I was gentle. I went like that. *(He slaps her)*

MRS SLOCOMBE You didn't. You went like that. *(She gives him a hard slap)*

PEACOCK I do not go like that. *(He gives her a hard slap)*

MRS SLOCOMBE Well, next time I shall go like that. *(She slaps him)*

PEACOCK In which case, I shall go like that. *(He slaps her)*

MRS SLOCOMBE Two can play at that game. *(She slaps him again)*

RUMBOLD Stop, stop, please.

MRS SLOCOMBE *and* PEACOCK *have to be separated.*

Forgetting that unfortunate incident, sir, what do you think?

MR GRACE What do I think—I think you've all done very well. So close the shop, Mr Rumbold, and off you all go on your holidays.

They cheer and RUMBOLD *plays again. They dance again.*

Curtain.

ACT II

The Reception at the Don Bernardo Hotel.

There is one counter, behind which is a large artist's illustration of how the annexe will look.

The group enter in their holiday gear, led by **RUMBOLD** *and* **PEACOCK**. **MRS SLOCOMBE** *and* **MISS BRAHMS**, *wearing dark glasses, have two balloons each. Under each balloon hangs a sign saying "Hotel Don Bernardo".*

MRS SLOCOMBE Doesn't it give you the holiday spirit when they give you balloons at the airport.

MISS BRAHMS They're not giving nothing away. They're advertising their hotel.

RUMBOLD They didn't give any to the men.

HUMPHRIES *enters with one, long balloon.*

MISS BRAHMS Mr Humphries got one.

HUMPHRIES Mine was a consolation prize.

LUCAS *arrives. He is carrying* **MRS SLOCOMBE**'s *wig on a wig head. It is in fact a ventriloquist dummy.*

MRS SLOCOMBE Do be careful of my wig, Mr Lucas. It's my evening hair, you know.

LUCAS *(to the head)* What do you think of the trip so far?

HEAD Rubbish.

RUMBOLD Ring the bell, Peacock.

PEACOCK I hope you're not going to continue to order me about. We are on holiday, you know.

RUMBOLD I'm sorry. Ring the bell, Stephen.

PEACOCK *rings the bell.*

DON BERNARDO *enters.*

BERNARDO Ah, señor, señorita—welcome, welcome.

He embraces RUMBOLD *and kisses him on both cheeks. He does likewise to* PEACOCK *and* GRAINGER. *Meanwhile,* HUMPHRIES *takes out a mirror and combs his hair in anticipation.* DON BERNARDO *passes* HUMPHRIES, *he embraces* MISS BRAHMS. MRS SLOCOMBE *is waiting eagerly—he shakes her hand.* HUMPHRIES *runs to the end of the line.* DON BERNARDO *embraces* HUMPHRIES.

HUMPHRIES He had me worried there for a minute.

BERNARDO I am most honoured to welcome you to the Don Bernardo Palace Hotel. Who are you, please?

PEACOCK I believe you have a booking in the name of Grace Brothers.

BERNARDO Of course, señor. You are the Grace Brothers?

PEACOCK That is correct. Si.

BERNARDO And the ladies?

PEACOCK They are the Grace Brothers as well.

BERNARDO The ladies are brothers? Ah, I am hearing about this. You are the English drag act—no? Now I look I can see. *(He crosses to* MRS SLOCOMBE*)* These are the balloons. Very funny. *(He is about to test* MRS SLOCOMBE*'s bosom)*

MRS SLOCOMBE Get off. Captain Peacock, will you tell him that I object to being ravaged like this.

RUMBOLD I think I should explain. We are all employed by Grace Brothers department store. We have a booking at this hotel for seven rooms.

PEACOCK Siette chambres.

RUMBOLD Thank you, Peacock.

BERNARDO Yes, you have booking. *(He shows him the book)* Grace Brothers—two brothers—one room—two beds.

RUMBOLD *(to* PEACOCK*)* I think one has to assert one's authority here, Peacock. Now see here, I want to see the manager.

BERNARDO I am the manager. But there is nothing to worry about, señor. We do have rooms for you.

RUMBOLD Ah—that's better.

BERNARDO Tomorrow.

ALL Tomorrow!

MRS SLOCOMBE What about tonight?

BERNARDO Tonight I can only give you the annexe.

HUMPHRIES *(seeing the illustration)* All those little cottages— doesn't it look nice.

BERNARDO Yes, señor. Very nice. They is being built next year.

PEACOCK Next year. What about tonight?

BERNARDO Tonight I can only be giving you the pentyhouses.

PEACOCK Penthouses. That sounds all right.

MRS SLOCOMBE By—he had me worried there for a minute.

RUMBOLD Very well, then. We will all take a penthouse.

BERNARDO *(clapping his hands)* Conchita!

A very pretty dark Spanish girl, wearing a very short skirt, enters.

Conchita—the Grace Brothers.

CONCHITA *shakes hands with* **PEACOCK, RUMBOLD, LUCAS** *and* **GRAINGER.** *She embraces* **MRS SLOCOMBE** *and* **MISS BRAHMS.** **HUMPHRIES** *holds out his hand but gets embraced.*

HUMPHRIES Now you're getting me confused.

BERNARDO Conchita, the pentyhouses.

CONCHITA *picks up* **PEACOCK***'s case and shows her pants.*

PEACOCK Yes, I'm looking forward to seeing the pantyhoses. I mean the pentyhouses.

They go off, leaving **DON BERNARDO.**

CESAR *enters swiftly.*

CESAR Bernardo.

BERNARDO What are you doing here?

CESAR The revolution will start tomorrow. You must hide me tonight.

BERNARDO Go away, Cesar. I'm a man of peace. I don't want no trouble.

CESAR You have a room?

BERNARDO Yes, one room only—but it is not for you.

CESAR brings out his gun.

Upstairs, first on the right.

CESAR You make up your mind, Bernardo. You are with them or you are with us.

BERNARDO I am with you.

CESAR So I sleep here tonight, and where is your beautiful serving girl Conchita?

BERNARDO Conchita? She is not for you, Cesar, she is for me.

CESAR   But you tell me every night she bolt the door of her bedroom against you.

BERNARDO   But tonight will be different.

CESAR   How you knowing this?

BERNARDO   *(producing the bolt)* I take off the bolt.

CESAR   But tomorrow I may die. Tonight I must have woman.

BERNARDO   You are in luck. There are two beautiful English women, pale skin, big boobidoos. Look, I show you picture. *(He picks up the passports)*

CESAR *takes one of them.*

CESAR   Ah, very good, the name Bumphries.

BERNARDO   No, Cesar, this the one, look at this. Mrs Slocombe. *(He shows* MRS SLOCOMBE's *holiday snap)*

CESAR   Ho ho, the face... *(He indicates half and half)* But the body—ho ho. Tonight you will tell me where she sleep.

BERNARDO   I will—tonight she is yours. I give her to you.

The lights cross-fade as we open the tabs to reveal the walled patio of the hotel. The back part of the patio is on a raised area and on it are five tents. Two tents are on a lower area. Entrance from the hotel is right.

The Grace Brothers party enter and survey the scene, led by CONCHITA.

MRS SLOCOMBE   Oh, this must be the garden area. I wonder what these tents are for.

LUCAS   Probably for the contractors building the annexe.

PEACOCK   *(looking up)* I wonder how one gets up to the pentyhouses.

MISS BRAHMS   *(pointing)* Oh, look, they've got a big one of these balloons flying up over the hotel.

As she points, we see a winding handle connected to a rope which goes up out of sight.

RUMBOLD *(indicating* **CONCHITA***)* Ask her, Peacock.

CONCHITA *bends to put the cases down.*

PEACOCK How does one get up the pantyhoses—er, I mean *donde* the penthouses.

CONCHITA Aqui. *(A key)*

RUMBOLD I beg your pardon?

CONCHITA *(starting to go)* Aqui, aqui.

MRS SLOCOMBE If we need the key don't stand there—go and get one.

CONCHITA *exits.*

RUMBOLD Quite a simple language really.

PEACOCK Aqui means here.

RUMBOLD Well, I can't see any penthouses.

As they look round **DON BERNARDO** *arrives.*

PEACOCK Excuse me, Don Bernardo.

BERNARDO Ah, the Grace Brothers. *(He embraces* **PEACOCK** *and* **GRAINGER** *again)*

GRAINGER Now don't start all that again.

MRS SLOCOMBE Why? We're not in a hurry.

PEACOCK We've had a long journey. We're hot and tired and we'd like a nice bath, shower and comfortable beds in our penthouses—where are they?

BERNARDO You have one pentyhouse each.

RUMBOLD Good.

BERNARDO *(gesturing to the row of tents)* There they is.

PEACOCK What are you talking about? Those are not penthouses.

BERNARDO What are you talking about—of course they are pentyhouses. Look, I show you. Take a penty pole and penty pegs. Put it up, what do you get? A pentyhouse.

RUMBOLD He means tents.

BERNARDO (*slapping his forehead*) Of course, tentehouses. My English spelling is so bad. Whenever I'm wanting T I'm having a P.

HUMPHRIES (*to* LUCAS) Remind me to stick to coffee.

MISS BRAHMS Tents! You won't catch me in a tent.

LUCAS I'd have a better chance.

MRS SLOCOMBE Captain Peacock, as you have some Spanish, will you tell this person we are not kipping under canvas and I'm unanimous in this.

PEACOCK Er, look, we have booked seven rooms in this hotel and we have confirmation.

BERNARDO You have confirmation, but we not get the rooms till tomorrow.

GRAINGER Can't we go somewhere else?

BERNARDO Town full.

RUMBOLD We'd better have a conference, Peacock.

PEACOCK *nods and steps away from* DON BERNARDO *with* RUMBOLD.

PEACOCK Are you free, Mrs Slocombe, Miss Brahms... Over here.

They join him.

Mr Grainger, are you free?

GRAINGER *glances around.*

GRAINGER Yes, I'm free.

PEACOCK Mr Lucas, are you and Mr Humphries free?

HUMPHRIES Very free, Captain Peacock.

They gather round.

PEACOCK Now we appear to have a bit of a crisis on our hands. Obviously we are in the right but due to circumstances beyond our control, we are left with two alternatives. Either to sleep on the beach or sleep here.

GRAINGER Or go home.

PEACOCK Yes, or go home.

BERNARDO No planes.

PEACOCK As I was saying, two alternatives.

BERNARDO Please, I'm sorry, but you stay here—you have beautiful food now—and the beautiful wine—you sleep in the beautiful tent—and tomorrow you have your beautiful rooms—what do you say?

HUMPHRIES If we say yes, do we get another kiss?

RUMBOLD Hands up those who want us to stay.

All put their hands up, including **DON BERNARDO**.

BERNARDO *(clapping hands and calling)* Conchita, the dinner.

CONCHITA *appears pushing a table on wheels. It already has the food on it. If special effects on the table are required, a table cloth hanging down at the side could conceal an operator.*

(indicating a pile of chairs) Take for yourself each a seat.

They do so.

HUMPHRIES We'd better start learning the language. What's Spanish for seat?

BERNARDO Asinto.

HUMPHRIES That's easy to remember.

DON BERNARDO *goes to get the wine.*

GRAINGER I must say, I'm feeling very peckish. All I had in the aeroplane was a dead thing in jelly.

They start to sit.

MRS SLOCOMBE Oh, doesn't the food look different.

MISS BRAHMS Smells different too.

GRAINGER Certainly a nice change from the staff canteen. I hope it's good.

HUMPHRIES Well, two hundred flies can't be wrong. Get off. *(He waves his hand)*

PEACOCK *(picking up a bowl)* Well, let's tuck in... Who's for melon balls?

HUMPHRIES *(putting his hand up)* Me.

PEACOCK *passes the bowl. They all select something.*

PEACOCK I think I'll try the seafood salad.

LUCAS That's supposed to make you virile, isn't it?

PEACOCK I hardly think two mussels and a shrivelled-up prawn will affect my sex life one way or the other.

MRS SLOCOMBE Oh, I must say this salad tastes lovely.

MISS BRAHMS Oh, ain't the insects greedy round here.

MRS SLOCOMBE What do you mean?

MISS BRAHMS That green wriggly thing's just picked up some of your salad, put it on its back and now he's marching off with it.

MRS SLOCOMBE *(putting on her glasses)* Oh, what a whopper. *(She takes a spoon and hammers at the adversary)*

HUMPHRIES Tough little monkeys, aren't they?

MRS SLOCOMBE *finally mashes it to death.*

MRS SLOCOMBE That's put me right off.

HUMPHRIES I'll bet it's given him a bit of a headache too.

DON BERNARDO *returns.*

BERNARDO Now for you we have the special dish of the house— Pulpo Langosta Grande. *(With a flourish, he removes the big lid from a dish to reveal a giant lobster with open claws)*

Gasps of appreciation from the others.

MISS BRAHMS What a whopper.

BERNARDO And finally the speciality of the casa.

HUMPHRIES Funny thing to have a speciality of—

BERNARDO Pulpo Grande. *(He takes the lid off another large dish)*

MRS SLOCOMBE What's that?

BERNARDO Big octapussy. Now you tuck in and enjoy while I get the wine.

DON BERNARDO *exits.*

They sit staring hypnotised at the bowl as a black tentacle appears, waves about, then points to MRS SLOCOMBE, *then beckons her. They all hit it with long bread rolls and force the lid back on.*

HUMPHRIES I'll tell you this, I'm not going swimming.

PEACOCK Perhaps we should turn our attention to the lobster.

RUMBOLD *(anxiously)* I hope it's fresh.

MISS BRAHMS Give it a sniff.

RUMBOLD *stands, bends over, a claw grabs him by the tie, pulls him down and the other claw snips at his nose.*

RUMBOLD Get it off, get it off.

GRAINGER *produces a pair of scissors from his top pocket. He snips off the tie.* **RUMBOLD** *collapses back in his chair.*

You cut my tie.

LUCAS We thought you were losing, sir.

DON BERNARDO *enters, carrying a Spanish wine jug with a long spout and a big goblet.*

BERNARDO El Vino for the Grace Brothers. First the Goblet of Honour for the Body Beautiful. *(He places the goblet in front of* **MRS SLOCOMBE***)*

MRS SLOCOMBE Oh, aren't they gallant. Muchas gracias.

BERNARDO Ah, you speak Spanish.

MRS SLOCOMBE Un petit peu.

DON BERNARDO *holds the wine jug and starts to pour into the goblet. He raises the wine jug higher and higher, making a long stream of wine which goes on for a long time. (Maybe we have a receptacle connected to the goblet under the table) They all start to move uncomfortably.* **PEACOCK** *and* **HUMPHRIES** *cross and uncross their legs.*

Captain Peacock, have you got your phrase book?

PEACOCK *(looking at the book)* Yes.

MRS SLOCOMBE What's Spanish for "Where's the little girls' room"?

PEACOCK I'm already ahead of you, Mrs Slocombe. Donde estan los servicios.

BERNARDO *(pointing with a free hand to a wooden hut)* Over there, señor.

MRS SLOCOMBE Thank you...

There is a brief pause, then there is a concerted rush towards the little hut. **MRS SLOCOMBE** *gets to the top of the steps first and pauses at the door, which is round the back away from the audience.*

Ladies first. *(She enters and closes the door)*

They start to return to the table. **MRS SLOCOMBE** *pops her head round the side of the hut.*

HUMPHRIES That was quick.

MRS SLOCOMBE There's no bolt.

BERNARDO In Spain when it is occupied, we sing.

MRS SLOCOMBE I see. *(She disappears)*

There is a moment's silence. Then she sings the first line of "AH SWEET MYSTERY". They all join in, singing the next two lines. **MRS SLOCOMBE** *pops her head up through the roof skylight of the hut.*

Belt up, you're putting me off. *(She disappears)*

LUCAS Sorry, Mrs Slocombe, we'll sing something else.

ALL *(singing)*

EVERY TIME IT RAINS, IT RAINS, PENNIES FROM HEAVEN...

A hand comes through a hole in side of the hut and pulls the chain which is extended outside. Loud flush. The hut shakes violently. **MRS SLOCOMBE** *emerges and tries to compose herself.*

RUMBOLD Let's sample the wine, shall we? *(He starts to pour)*

MRS SLOCOMBE *returns to the table.*

MRS SLOCOMBE For some reason best known to the Spanish, the bolt is on the outside.

LUCAS Well, if they like the song, they keep you there and make you do it again. *(He produces a pencil and starts to write on a paper napkin)*

RUMBOLD Composing a letter to send to your mother, Mr Lucas?

LUCAS No, sir, it's for Shirley there—I'm giving her one last chance and if she doesn't agree to what I'm suggesting, I'll have to start chatting up the Spanish crumpet.

RUMBOLD What exactly are you suggesting?

LUCAS *(reading)* Dear sexy knickers, I've been mad about you ever since we met. Come to my tent tonight and we'll watch the moon rise together.

RUMBOLD She won't fall for that, will she?

LUCAS If she doesn't, it's the last chance she'll get and the Spanish crumpet can have me all to themselves. *(He waves to attract* CONCHITA's *attention as she pours wine)*

She comes over to him. During the following the others speak amongst themselves.

Do you speak English?

CONCHITA *(bending)* A leetle titty bit.

LUCAS Give this note to señorita with the spectacles.

CONCHITA Si, señor.

As CONCHITA *crosses,* MRS SLOCOMBE *puts her glasses on to look at her wine.* MISS BRAHMS *takes her dark glasses off, and gazes at the sky.*

MISS BRAHMS It's getting quite dark.

MRS SLOCOMBE The nights clamp down very early in the tropicals.

MISS BRAHMS *turns away to talk to* MR HUMPHRIES. CONCHITA *gives the note to* MRS SLOCOMBE.

CONCHITA For you, señorita.

Looking away from **LUCAS***'s end of the table,* **MRS SLOCOMBE** *removes her glasses.*

MRS SLOCOMBE A note? How very mysterious. Who sent it?

CONCHITA The señor who pour wine now. *(She moves away)*

LUCAS *who has been pouring the wine hands the bottle to* **PEACOCK.**

LUCAS Fill her up, Captain Peacock.

MRS SLOCOMBE *gives her glasses a quick polish. By the time she turns and puts on her glasses and focuses,* **PEACOCK** *has the bottle.*

MRS SLOCOMBE *(reacting)* Ooh, Captain Peacock. *(She turns and taps* **MISS BRAHMS** *on the shoulder)*

MISS BRAHMS *turns.*

Miss Brahms, Captain Peacock has sent me a note.

MISS BRAHMS Ooh, what's it say?

MRS SLOCOMBE I'm just about to read it. *(She reads)* "Dear sexy knickers".

MISS BRAHMS *(laughing)* I didn't know you wore sexy knickers.

MRS SLOCOMBE Miss Brahms, some people find directoires very exciting. At least they did in the war.

MISS BRAHMS Go on, then.

MRS SLOCOMBE *(reading)* "I've been mad about you ever since we met. Come to my tent tonight and we'll watch the"... *(She peers, puzzled)* What rise together? Oh, moon. Well, would you believe it? *(She turns and looks at* **PEACOCK***)*

PEACOCK *raises his glass.* **MRS SLOCOMBE** *raises hers.*

Ooh, don't they get bold in the tropics.

MISS BRAHMS You're not going, are you?

MRS SLOCOMBE Well—I—I think I will, just to teach him a lesson. I shall lead him on, then I shall give him a piece of my mind—eventually—give me something to write with. *(She gets a napkin)*

MISS BRAHMS *produces a pencil from her handbag.*

MISS BRAHMS It's my eyebrow pencil.

MRS SLOCOMBE *(dictating aloud as she writes)* Dear sexy Y-fronts, will come to your tent after dark and together we'll see it come up.

She calls to **BERNARDO** *who is busy round the table.*

Bernardo.

BERNARDO Si, señorita.

MRS SLOCOMBE Would you give this note privito to the man with the moustache at the end of the tabelo.

BERNARDO Si, señorita.

DON BERNARDO *takes the note and taps* **PEACOCK** *on the shoulder.*

Señor, a note from the señorita down there.

PEACOCK Which one is that?

BERNARDO The one with the figure like Raquel Welch.

DON BERNARDO *exits.*

PEACOCK *(to himself turning away from* **LUCAS***)* Ah, a note from Miss Brahms. *(He mouths without using his voice)* "Dear Sexy Y-fronts". *(He pauses, then pulls at his trouser band to check his underwear. He continues to mouth the message to the end. Then, aloud)* Watch what come up? I wonder what she has in mind.

MISS BRAHMS Bottoms up, Captain Peacock.

PEACOCK There's no accounting for taste. Well, it's a new one on me. *(He takes a pen, gets a napkin and writes)* Can't wait to get together with you tonight. More discreet if I come to your tent. Bottoms up. Stephen.

PEACOCK gets up and stops CONCHITA on his way to the loo. At this moment, MISS BRAHMS holds up a mirror and starts putting on lipstick.

Conchita.

CONCHITA Si, señor.

PEACOCK Give this to one making up face in mirror.

CONCHITA Si, señor. *(She takes the note)*

PEACOCK continues towards the loo. As MISS BRAHMS finishes applying lipstick, MR HUMPHRIES borrows her mirror.

HUMPHRIES May I? *(He takes a comb and does his hair)*

CONCHITA arrives at the table.

I look as if I've been dragged through a hedge backwards.

CONCHITA This is for you. *(She gives him the note)*

HUMPHRIES Ooh, a billy do. *(He starts to read and reacts)* I would never have guessed in a thousand years.

We hear PEACOCK from the loo as he sings the first two lines of "AH SWEET MYSTERY" in a deep voice. They all join in the song except HUMPHRIES who gets up, crosses to the loo and pulls the outside chain. There is a yell from within. The hut shakes. HUMPHRIES returns to the table.

That should dampen his ardour.

Black-out.

*The tabs draw. The reception desk comes in. The lights
come up on the reception area.*

CONCHITA *is on the phone.*

CONCHITA Ci quero una conferencia con cobro revertido. Inglese.

HUMPHRIES *enters.*

HUMPHRIES Has my call to England come through yet?

CONCHITA He just come.

HUMPHRIES *(taking the phone)* It's my mother, she worries
about me, you know. *(Into the phone)* Hello, Mother...oh,
we've only got as far as Bootle, still, it's only a short walk.
Yes, I'll hold.

CONCHITA Please, you must help me. I am in trouble.

HUMPHRIES Are you? *(Into the phone)* Yes, I'm still here.

CONCHITA It is Bernardo. He wants to... *(She whispers in his ear)*

HUMPHRIES Does he? *(Into the phone)* There's a lot of
interference going on and I don't know if it's your end or
mine.

CONCHITA *kneels pleading and throws her arms round
his waist.*

Quite a lot of it is mine.

CONCHITA He has taken the bolt from my door. Let me sleep
in your tent, I know I can trust you.

HUMPHRIES How did you work that out? *(Into the phone)* Hallo,
Mother, it's me... Yes, I told the pilot what you said and he
was very careful... Yes, I know I left my hot water bottle.

CONCHITA *stands and hugs him.*

I don't think I'm going to need it.

CONCHITA Oh, señor, tell me I may sleep with you. Bernardo
has taken the bolt off my door.

HUMPHRIES What do you say, Mother? ...Yes, you're right, it was a girl's voice... What's that? ...You're right, the change will do me good.

BERNARDO *(offstage, shouting)* Conchita, where are you?

CONCHITA *runs a few paces and listens anxiously.*

HUMPHRIES I'd better get off now. I don't want to run up a big bill.

CONCHITA *runs back to* **HUMPHRIES.**

CONCHITA Please say yes.

HUMPHRIES *(into the phone)* Give us a kiss then.

CONCHITA *thinks he means her.*

CONCHITA Oh, you beautiful man. *(She gives him a smacking kiss)*

HUMPHRIES *(to* **CONCHITA***)* Not you. *(Into the phone)* No, Mother, it was the night porter.

CONCHITA *(making to leave)* I'll see you in your tent tonight.

HUMPHRIES *(into the phone)* Yes, he has got a high voice. They slide down the banisters a lot round here... Yes, I'll remember to say my prayers...yes, I'll ask him to make me a good boy—mind you, he'll have his work cut out tonight... Goodbye. *(He hangs up)*

DON BERNARDO *enters.*

BERNARDO Buenas noches, señor—is your tent to your liking? You have got everything you need?

HUMPHRIES Yes, I think I shall have, one or two things I don't need. Look, for reasons I shan't go into, you don't happen to have a spare bed anywhere, do you?

BERNARDO There is one bed, señor, but I daren't let you have it.

HUMPHRIES *(taking out his wallet)* I'll make it worth your while.

BERNARDO *(confidentially)* The other bed is occupied by Cesar Rodrigues, the most feared man in all Spain... It is said he has killed twelve men with his bare hands.

HUMPHRIES If anybody wants me, I'll be in my tent.

HUMPHRIES *exits.*

CESAR *enters.*

CESAR Any messages for me?

BERNARDO No, all is quiet. Tomorrow is your big day.

CESAR And tonight is my big night. *(He picks up the photo of* **MRS SLOCOMBE** *and stares at it)* What a body. Now tell me which tent is she in?

BERNARDO I will show you myself...later. *(He produces a bottle of aftershave)* Tonight is also my big night. *(He slaps the aftershave on)*

CESAR What is that?

BERNARDO It's called Old Venice.

CESAR I also have need of Old Venice.

He takes the aftershave and applies it as **DON BERNARDO** *produces a bottle and two glasses from behind the counter and pours.*

BERNARDO Well, to the revolution.

CESAR To the revolution—but most of all to love. *(He kisses the photo)*

Black-out.

In the darkness, the tabs open on the tents. They are now downstage right behind the Number One tabs. From left to right the tents are occupied by **MISS BRAHMS,** *then* **MRS SLOCOMBE.** *The loo is centre, centre right is* **MR PEACOCK,** *right is* **HUMPHRIES.** *Before the night* *lighting comes up,* GRAINGER'*s voice is heard singing* **"AH SWEET MYSTERY".**

The lights come up to reveal the tents. All the cast are in night attire. MISS BRAHMS *is in bed, reading a book, in curlers. The front of each tent is cut out.*

We see MRS SLOCOMBE *in her tent as she applies perfume from a spray. She sings the second line of the song.*

MRS SLOCOMBE *(singing)*

AH I HOPE THAT CAPTAIN PEACOCK LIKES MY PONG.

PEACOCK *in his tent is using his electric shaver. He sings the third line.*

PEACOCK *(singing)*

AH, I HOPE MISS BRAHMS CAN STAND THE STRESS OF WAITING, BUT WITH MY Y-FRONTS HOW CAN I GO WRONG.

GRAINGER *pulls the chain and comes into view.*

GRAINGER Any more dinners like that and I shall have to have a longer song.

GRAINGER *goes off in the direction of his unseen tent.*

DON BERNARDO *enters, goes to* PEACOCK'*s tent and enters.*

During their exchange, MRS SLOCOMBE *picks up her lilo and removes the plug to put more air in it.*

BERNARDO Buenas noches, señor.

PEACOCK Buenas noches.

BERNARDO I forget to asking you. What time you like breakfast?

PEACOCK Speaking on behalf of the men, eight o'clock.

BERNARDO And the ladies?

PEACOCK I'd better enquire.

PEACOCK *goes with* DON BERNARDO *to the side of* MRS SLOCOMBE*'s tent. He stands between her tent and the loo.*

(calling) Mrs Slocombe.

MRS SLOCOMBE *blows a raspberry into the lilo.* PEACOCK *reacts.*

(glancing between the loo and the tent) Where are you, Mrs Slocombe?

MRS SLOCOMBE *blows another raspberry.*

(to the tent) I thought you were. I can call back later if you wish.

MRS SLOCOMBE *blows a further raspberry.*

Or indeed not at all.

MRS SLOCOMBE It's all right. I've got the stopper in now. Did somebody call?

PEACOCK It's me, Captain Peacock.

MRS SLOCOMBE *drops the lilo and gives a quick spray of perfume.*

MRS SLOCOMBE I was just putting more air in my lilo.

PEACOCK Ah, that explains a lot. I have Don Bernardo here—he wonders what time we would like breakfast.

MRS SLOCOMBE *(simpering)* Oh, aren't we taking rather a lot for granted, Captain Peacock.

PEACOCK No, no. They have breakfast on the brochure.

MRS SLOCOMBE Is there a nice view from there?

PEACOCK Would eight thirty be all right?

MRS SLOCOMBE I'll leave that to you, Stephen, naturally.

PEACOCK *(to* **DON BERNARDO***)* Eight thirty.

DON BERNARDO *exits.*

PEACOCK *starts stealthily towards* **MISS BRAHMS***'s tent. As he gets to it,* **MR HUMPHRIES** *appears in dressing-gown and pyjamas, carrying a sponge bag, with his hair in curlers.* **PEACOCK** *immediately turns about and goes to his own tent and switches his light out.* **MISS BRAHMS***'s is the only tent alight.*

MISS BRAHMS *(reading aloud)* It was dark in the jungle hut, the drugged coconut juice was having its effect as Captain Strangeways struggled against the bonds that bound him face to face against the nubile body of Princess Lala. Suddenly he was aware of something stirring.

At this moment a large caterpillar type woof-n-poof starts to crawl up one side of the inner part of the tent. **MISS BRAHMS** *breaks off and watches it. She picks up a large fly swatter and tries to swat it. It quickly completes its journey to the other side of the tent and disappears.* **MISS BRAHMS** *goes to* **MR HUMPHRIES***' tent.*

(hissing) Mr Humphries. *(She bangs on the tent with the fly swatter)*

MR HUMPHRIES*' light goes on to reveal* **MR HUMPHRIES** *with his arm raised holding a hairdrier like a gun.*

HUMPHRIES Captain Peacock, I must warn you that I'm armed and dangerous.

MISS BRAHMS It's me, Shirley—are you free?

HUMPHRIES Providing you've not got designs on the body.

MISS BRAHMS What do you think I am—the tattooed Lady? *(She comes in)* I'm in a bit of trouble.

HUMPHRIES There's a lot of it about.

MISS BRAHMS I'm worried about a little teeny weeny thing.

HUMPHRIES There's a lot of those about as well.

MISS BRAHMS It crawled into my tent and I came out in big goose bumps.

HUMPHRIES I can see, dear—some of them haven't gone down.

MISS BRAHMS Anyway, I wondered if I could sleep in your tent and you could sleep in mine.

HUMPHRIES What makes you think I like creepy—hang on a minute—on second thoughts, I'll accept your offer. *(He goes out, pops his head back)* It was teeny weeny, wasn't it?

MISS BRAHMS *(handing him the fly swatter)* Yes, but take this in case.

HUMPHRIES *gives her the hairdrier.*

HUMPHRIES You'd better have this, you might need a weapon.

MISS BRAHMS *turns the light out and* HUMPHRIES *goes to* MISS BRAHMS'*s tent. Raising the fly swatter, he enters and looks around. As he bends looking, a number of woof-n-poofs appear going up the tent wall beside him... He spots them and swipes at them with the swatter. He backs out of the tent. As he hesitates, the lights come up on* MRS SLOCOMBE'*s tent. She pulls up her nightie to reveal her Union Jack directoire knickers.*

MRS SLOCOMBE "Dear Sexy Knickers". How romantic. *(She takes out the note)* What did he say again. "Come to my tent and we'll watch the moon rise together". *(She creeps out of her tent and heads for* CAPTAIN PEACOCK'*s. She sees* HUMPHRIES*)*

As he approaches, they bump into each other and react.

I was just—er—taking a little walk. I usually give my pussy an airing at about this time.

HUMPHRIES Do you mind if I stay in your tent till you come back?

MRS SLOCOMBE Whatever for?

HUMPHRIES Well, I was in Miss Brahms's tent and there was a big furry thing that frightened me.

MRS SLOCOMBE What was it?

HUMPHRIES I don't know. I haven't seen one before so I hit it with this. *(He shows the fly swatter)*

MRS SLOCOMBE And where's Miss Brahms now?

HUMPHRIES Last time I saw her she was looking for her tranquilizers.

MRS SLOCOMBE I'm not surprised. Why can't you sleep in your tent?

HUMPHRIES I've put Miss Brahms in there.

MRS SLOCOMBE Well, if she's gone to your tent she must have liked it.

HUMPHRIES No, she didn't, but she told me it was only a little one, but when I saw it, it was a great big one, I thought it was going to bite me.

MRS SLOCOMBE You poor mixed-up boy. You go into my tent and when I get back I'll explain things to you.

HUMPHRIES Thank you. Can I borrow your face cream?

MRS SLOCOMBE Of course. And help yourself to the vitamin tablets.

HUMPHRIES *goes into* **MRS SLOCOMBE**'s *tent and the Light goes down.* **MRS SLOCOMBE** *arrives outside* **PEACOCK**'s *tent. Light up on* **PEACOCK**'s *tent. He is applying aftershave as he sings the first line of "TONIGHT" from "West Side Story".* **MRS SLOCOMBE** *replies with the second line of the song.*

PEACOCK I didn't know Shirley was a contralto. *(He looks puzzled)*

MRS SLOCOMBE *(whispering)* Are you there, Stephen?

PEACOCK Yes, I was just about to come to your tent.

MRS SLOCOMBE Impetuous boy.

PEACOCK Are you sure nobody's seen you?

MRS SLOCOMBE They will do if I'm stuck here much longer.

PEACOCK *(picking up his dressing-gown)* Just a minute.

As MRS SLOCOMBE *waits,* RUMBOLD *enters in his dressing-gown.*

MRS SLOCOMBE *sees him and rushes into the loo.* PEACOCK *now has his dressing-gown on. Just as* RUMBOLD *passes* PEACOCK*'s tent,* PEACOCK *calls.*

Pssst.

RUMBOLD *stops in his tracks. A hand comes to the side of* PEACOCK*'s tent and a finger beckons* RUMBOLD. RUMBOLD *blinks, takes a couple of paces away and stops again.*

Pssst.

The finger beckons again. RUMBOLD *frowns and cautiously enters* PEACOCK*'s tent. He comes up behind* PEACOCK, *who is still beckoning.*

(hissing) Where are you?

RUMBOLD I'm here.

PEACOCK *(startled, turning)* Mr Rumbold!

RUMBOLD What are you doing, Peacock?

PEACOCK What do you mean what am I doing?

RUMBOLD Your finger was beckoning.

PEACOCK *(holding up a finger)* Oh, you mean this finger, sir.

RUMBOLD Yes, it was doing a sort of "come hither" like that. *(He demonstrates)*

PEACOCK Ah yes, I can explain that. I was trying to attract someone's attention.

RUMBOLD You did. Mine.

PEACOCK Not yours, sir, it was, er... *(Inspired)* Room service.

RUMBOLD They won't see that in the dark.

PEACOCK Perhaps that's why they didn't come. Will there be anything else, sir?

RUMBOLD No, carry on, Peacock.

> RUMBOLD *exits, goes straight to the loo and enters.* MRS SLOCOMBE *screams. They both leap out into view.*

MRS SLOCOMBE *(shocked)* Mr Rumbold!

RUMBOLD I'm sorry but you're supposed to sing a song.

MRS SLOCOMBE I forgot the words.

RUMBOLD Well, you could have gone tiddle tiddle tum tum.

MRS SLOCOMBE Whether I wish to go tiddle tiddle or not is my business—good night, Mr Rumbold.

RUMBOLD Good night. *(He goes into the loo)*

> MRS SLOCOMBE *creeps round the back of* PEACOCK's *tent. At the same time* PEACOCK, *kneeling, is trying to peer through the crack in the side of the tent.* MRS SLOCOMBE *appears behind* PEACOCK *and taps him on the shoulder. She raises her nightie and exposes one directoire-encased leg.*

PEACOCK *(kneeling)* Mr Rumbold? *(He turns and sees the leg)* Mr Humphries? *(He looks up)* Mrs Slocombe!

MRS SLOCOMBE I've got them on.

PEACOCK I'm glad to hear it.

MRS SLOCOMBE Mr Rumbold caught me in the loo and told me off for not tiddling.

PEACOCK Rather exceeding his authority I should have thought.

MRS SLOCOMBE I'm not serious about your Y-fronts, you know—

PEACOCK Good.

MRS SLOCOMBE I'm not that sort of girl at all. What time is it?

PEACOCK Eleven thirty.

MRS SLOCOMBE What time does it come up, then?

PEACOCK Well, er—

MRS SLOCOMBE My friend Mrs Axelby says it looks much bigger in the tropics.

PEACOCK Really?

MRS SLOCOMBE I suppose if you were in the Arctic it would be small.

PEACOCK That would follow.

MRS SLOCOMBE Oh, isn't it romantic—you, me—a hot Spanish night. *(She starts to put her arms round him)* All that's missing is the music.

As she goes to kiss a horrified PEACOCK, *they freeze as* RUMBOLD *sings "AH SWEET MYSTERY".*

PEACOCK *collapses in her embrace. As he runs off, pursued by* MRS SLOCOMBE, *the light goes out in that tent.*

Spot on GRAINGER *entering in dressing-gown with a sponge bag. He pauses by the loo.*

The singing stops after the first four lines.

GRAINGER If there's going to be another verse, I'll come back later.

RUMBOLD *starts to sing again.*

Oh, damn.

GRAINGER *exits back in the same direction. As he does so,* CONCHITA *enters.*

She goes into HUMPHRIES' *tent in which* MISS BRAHMS *is asleep.* CONCHITA *pauses by the bed, turns her back to* MISS BRAHMS, *and starts to undress.* MISS BRAHMS *sits up.*

CONCHITA All the time here I am being chased by that terrible sexy man, I feel safe with you—take me to England and let me live with you. *(She turns and gets into bed with* MISS BRAHMS*)*

MISS BRAHMS 'Ere, what are you playing at?

CONCHITA *jumps out, surprised.*

(offended) I'm not one of those.

CONCHITA I'm sorry, I want to sleep with Mr Humphries. He will make me happy.

MISS BRAHMS You'll be lucky. *(She points)* He's in the one at the other end.

As CONCHITA *dresses* LUCAS *enters in pyjamas and goes to* MISS BRAHMS's *tent which is empty.*

LUCAS *(whispering)* Shirley. *(He looks in)* I'm early. I'll get in and pretend I'm a hot water bottle. *(He gets into bed)*

CONCHITA *arrives outside the tent.*

CONCHITA *(whispering)* Are you there, Mr Bumfreeze?

LUCAS Who is it?

CONCHITA It is Conchita, Mr Bumfreeze. Can I come in?

LUCAS It depends what you want.

CONCHITA I want to spend the night with you.

LUCAS *(à la* HUMPHRIES*)* I'm free.

CONCHITA *enters and* LUCAS *hides under the sheet. He pops his head out as she undresses with her back to him as before.*

CONCHITA All the time I am being chased by that terrible sexy man Don Bernardo. I feel safe with you, take me to England and let me stay with you.

LUCAS *pops back out of sight as she lifts the sheet and jumps in with him. As soon as she gets into the bed, a woof-n-poof appears, climbs down the tent pole, up the bed leg and under the sheet.*

(from under the sheet) Oh, Mr Bunfreeze—Oh, Mr Bumfphries—

With a concerted yell LUCAS *and* CONCHITA *both jump out of bed and run off.*

We fade the light on that tent. The light comes up on MR HUMPHRIES *in* MRS SLOCOMBE*'s tent. He sits on the bed or stool, looking through her make-up box, taking out bottles.*

HUMPHRIES *(reading bottles)* Let's see—what she's got. Anti-wrinkle cream. I don't need that, not on my face anyway, on my elbows maybe. *(He takes a large bottle of Badedas. He reads)* Anything can happen with Badedas. *(He puts a bit behind each ear)*

DON BERNARDO *and* CESAR *enter.*

BERNARDO *(pointing)* There you are, Cesar—the tent of Mrs Slocombe.

CESAR *(holding the photo)* The one with the beautiful body.

BERNARDO That's right, good luck.

CESAR Good luck to you, amigo.

BERNARDO *(producing the bolt)* I don't need luck. I have the bolt.

DON BERNARDO *exits.*

CESAR *approaches the tent containing* MR HUMPHRIES.

CESAR *(hissing)* Pssst.

HUMPHRIES Go away, Captain Peacock. Any impressions that
I have given you that I would welcome your advances are
entirely false—and I wish it to be known by the world.

GRAINGER *sings the first three lines of "RULE
BRITANNIA" from the loo.* HUMPHRIES *stands and
salutes.*

That was a quick one.

CESAR I am not Peacock, my name is Cesar.

HUMPHRIES Not the one that killed the twelve people with
his bare hands.

CESAR The same.

HUMPHRIES Oh, Mother...

CESAR I saw the photograph in your passport and you have
set me aflame.

HUMPHRIES It wasn't even a good one.

CESAR I have lost my heart to you, dear beautiful Mrs Slocombe.

HUMPHRIES *(mouthing)* Mrs Slocombe.

CESAR Are you going to invite me into your tent?

HUMPHRIES It's not very convenient. *(During the following, he
dons* MRS SLOCOMBE*'s wig and a dress, or wrap)*

CESAR Why? Have you a man in there?

HUMPHRIES Oh no no no.

CESAR If I find a man in there I will cut his throat. Please tell
me you're alone.

HUMPHRIES I'm free, I'm alone.

CESAR Now do you invite me in or do I rip it open with my bare hands?

HUMPHRIES You don't give a girl much choice, do you?

CESAR I come in.

HUMPHRIES Hold on, there's a couple of things I've got to attend to. *(He takes* **MRS SLOCOMBE**'s *balloons and stuffs them down the front of his dress)*

CESAR Are you ready?

HUMPHRIES Yes, but only for a chat.

> **CESAR** *enters, with dagger.*

Oh, put that thing away.

CESAR You do not like the cold steel.

HUMPHRIES I don't even like cold tripe.

CESAR I expect you are wondering why I am here.

HUMPHRIES I've got a pretty good idea.

CESAR *(showing the photo)* I'm here because of this, the camera cannot lie.

HUMPHRIES *(taking it)* It's telling a bit of a fib this time.

CESAR You are a woman in a million.

HUMPHRIES I'm even more unusual than that.

CESAR Tomorrow I may die but tonight will be a night to remember.

HUMPHRIES Wouldn't you rather go down the pub with the boys? It's happy time from ten till twelve.

CESAR Do not joke with me. I am Cesar, the revolutionary. I have six hundred men under me.

HUMPHRIES Well, what do you need me for, then?

CESAR puts his arm round HUMPHRIES *who breaks away.* CESAR *goes after him.*

CESAR Just one kiss.

HUMPHRIES Now control yourself. I'm not that sort of a girl. I was very strictly brought up.

CESAR But you have kissed a man before.

HUMPHRIES That's none of your business.

CESAR Is it my moustache that frightens you?

HUMPHRIES No, my Auntie Ethel has one. She used to wax the end with candle grease and light herself up for Christmas.

CESAR traps HUMPHRIES *and puts his arm around him.* HUMPHRIES *ducks away.*

CESAR You are a very slippery customer.

HUMPHRIES *runs out.*

You won't get away from me.

HUMPHRIES *arrives at* PEACOCK'*s tent.*

HUMPHRIES Captain Peacock, all is forgiven.

He runs through the tent, pursued by CESAR. *He goes to* MISS BRAHMS'*s tent, shouts "Help", runs through the tent containing* MISS BRAHMS, *who screams and sits up in her nightie.*

Help, there's a man after me.

MISS BRAHMS I'm not surprised, dressed like that.

HUMPHRIES *runs through the tent, followed by* CESAR. *He runs round the back of the loo and creeps to the other side.* CESAR *and* HUMPHRIES *on either side of the loo. They creep round, following each other. Then* CESAR *reverses direction, catches* HUMPHRIES *at the back and appears with him in his arms.*

CESAR Now I take you to my room.

HUMPHRIES And I thought Butlins was dangerous.

CESAR carries HUMPHRIES *out of sight offstage.*

We hear the bang of two balloons popping.

HUMPHRIES *appears and runs into* MRS SLOCOMBE.

MRS SLOCOMBE Mr Humphries...what are you doing in my wig and nightie?

HUMPHRIES I don't care if you bought it in Wigan or St Helens, there's a man after me.

MRS SLOCOMBE Get behind me.

CESAR appears, holding two burst balloons.

CESAR Where is she?

MRS SLOCOMBE Who?

CESAR *(waving the balloons)* Mrs Slocombe.

MRS SLOCOMBE I am Mrs Slocombe. What do you want?

HUMPHRIES He's after your balloons, dear.

CESAR opens his arms, starts singing "AH SWEET MYSTERY" and chases MRS SLOCOMBE *and* HUMPHRIES *offstage.*

Black-out. The lights come up on the reception scene. Morning.

DON BERNARDO *is behind the counter.*

CESAR enters, dressed for the revolution.

CESAR Goodbye, Bernardo, next time I see you, I will either be the Presidente or I will be dead.

BERNARDO Don't say that, Cesar.

CESAR Never mind—long live the revolution.

BERNARDO Yes—long live the revolution. By the way, the one with the body, did you have a night to remember?

CESAR It was a night that I shall never forget as long as I live.

TAERESA enters, a large fellow revolutionary, dressed in her uniform.

TAERESA *(urgently)* Cesar, Cesar. I have bad news. We failed to take the radio station and the Government troops have been alerted.

CESAR The fools.

TAERESA If we don't take the police headquarters, all is lost. You must come and lead the men yourself.

CESAR Bernardo—you must take a gun and fight by my side.

BERNARDO Cesar—there is nothing I would rather do but I must serve breakfast to the tourists. Besides, if you fail you will need somewhere to hide.

CESAR Bernardo, answer me truly. Are you still behind me?

BERNARDO Of course, but not so close.

TAERESA Come, Cesar, quickly.

CESAR and TAERESA exit.

CONCHITA enters with a tray piled with eggs, bacon, toast and marmalade, coffee, etc.

BERNARDO Conchita—I have been looking for you since sunrise—where did you spend the night?

CONCHITA I no tell.

BERNARDO Where are you going with that tray—and what is this? Eggs, bacon, toast, marmalade. That is not on the menu.

CONCHITA I know. Mr Lucas very hungry this morning.

BERNARDO Conchita, you should know better.

CONCHITA After one night with Mr Lucas I do know better.

BERNARDO How did it happen that this English pig found favour in your eyes?

CONCHITA I hid in my room but somebody had taken the bolt off the door.

The bell on the table rings offstage.

BERNARDO Hurry, the English want their breakfast.

She starts to go.

And Conchita, don't tell them about the revolution.

CONCHITA What revolution?

BERNARDO Cesar—he is trying again but it is not going well.

She starts to go again.

And Conchita—

CONCHITA Yes, Bernardo?

BERNARDO Don't forget to raise the balloon.

The lights cross-fade to the patio terrace. The table is set for breakfast. The balloon is down, showing the banner on which is written the name of the hotel.

PEACOCK *is seated with* **GRAINGER** *and* **LUCAS.**

RUMBOLD *enters.*

PEACOCK Good morning.

RUMBOLD Good morning.

PEACOCK Did you sleep well?

RUMBOLD Not entirely. There was a lot of to-ing and fro-ing in the night. I took a very strong sleeping pill and had a peculiar nightmare. Mrs Slocombe seemed to be assuring somebody she didn't know very well that whatever they did they wouldn't go off pop.

PEACOCK I too had a nightmare. I was being pursued by Mrs Slocombe. I then went to Miss Brahms's tent in response to a strange message I had received earlier, only to find Mr Humphries wearing a wig and Mrs Slocombe's nightdress, and shouting "get out, I'm going straight". Unfortunately I was awake.

GRAINGER Did you have a good night, Mr Lucas?

LUCAS Yes—marvellous, didn't sleep a wink.

CONCHITA *delivers the breakfast.*

Lovely grub.

PEACOCK What sort of night did you have, Mr Grainger?

GRAINGER I had an upset tummy. It made me rather hoarse. Looking at the menu I'd better rehearse the Mikado after lunch.

CONCHITA *winds up the balloon, showing much of her underwear.*

RUMBOLD What's that girl doing?

PEACOCK Advertising.

MISS BRAHMS *enters.*

LUCAS Hallo, Shirley—have a good night?

MISS BRAHMS I slept in Mr Humphries' tent.

RUMBOLD That's very encouraging.

MRS SLOCOMBE *enters.*

MISS BRAHMS Ooh, you look worn out.

MRS SLOCOMBE I am—I'm whacked. This man chased me miles up the beach.

LUCAS Did he get you?

MRS SLOCOMBE It was touch and go.

HUMPHRIES *enters dressed as a nun.*

HUMPHRIES *(singing)*
RAINDROPS ON ROSES AND WHISKERS ON KITTENS... *(He sits at the table)*

PEACOCK Mr Humphries—what possessed you?

HUMPHRIES A Spanish bandit very nearly did. I had to take sanctuary in a nunnery. I'd still be there if my needlework had been any good.

RUMBOLD I trust you won't be dressed like that for long.

HUMPHRIES I haven't taken the vows if that's what you're worried about.

MRS SLOCOMBE *notices her croissant against* MR LUCAS*'s large breakfast.*

MRS SLOCOMBE When's our breakfast arriving?

PEACOCK This is ours—one bun.

MRS SLOCOMBE Why the special treatment for Mr Lucas?

PEACOCK He's in training.

RUMBOLD *puts on a large beaknose nose shade.*

MRS SLOCOMBE Whatever's that?

RUMBOLD I'm worried about my nose.

LUCAS What about your ears?

MISS BRAHMS Well, I fancy getting on that beach for an hour. And then I'm going to have a go on one of those bicycle boats.

PEACOCK I shall try to find a golf course.

LUCAS What about you, Mr Grainger?

GRAINGER I shan't stray very far from the hotel.

A shot is heard off.

MRS SLOCOMBE Whatever's that?

PEACOCK Probably a shooting party.

A few more shots are heard.

MRS SLOCOMBE Do they get pheasants on the beach?

PEACOCK You get them anywhere.

We hear the sound of a plane diving and a machine gun burst.

MRS SLOCOMBE It's not very sporting to go after them with jet planes.

More shots off.

BERNARDO *runs in.*

BERNARDO I am sorry, señores. It is nothing to worry about. It is just a revolution. It will soon pass.

MRS SLOCOMBE Revolution? Ooh, fancy us being here for a revolution.

PEACOCK Well, I hope they're not going to charge extra for that.

MISS BRAHMS Well, I'm still going on the beach. *(She gets up)*

BERNARDO You cannot go out there. It is too dangerous.

MRS SLOCOMBE They're not fighting out there, are they?

BERNARDO According to the radio station, the rebels are retreating this way.

TAERESA *(offstage)* Conchita, Bernardo, come quickly.

BERNARDO *exits.*

MRS SLOCOMBE Well, what are we going to do?

LUCAS Perhaps Sister Humphries could say a few Hail Marys.

HUMPHRIES To think I could be in the New Forest camping with a friend.

RUMBOLD I wonder if there is anything on the radio.

MISS BRAHMS Hang on, I'll find out. *(She turns on her transistor)*

It squeaks a few times and there are a few snatches in a foreign language. Then we hear the BBC voice.

VOICE Australia 510 for two. The attempt to overthrow the government in Spain has met with unexpected opposition and the rebels are now in full retreat. All British subjects have taken refuge in the British embassies and consulates which are in no danger.

There is a burst of machine gunfire. Decorations and architectural features fall off the wall above the doors and windows.

MRS SLOCOMBE What do you mean safe? *(Into the radio)* We're not safe.

PEACOCK Steady on, Mrs Slocombe. The situation is perfectly plain. The troops out there are obviously not aware that we are British subjects. All we have to do is show the flag.

RUMBOLD We don't have a flag to show.

PEACOCK Without going into details, I happen to know that Mrs Slocombe has a nether garment which would serve our purpose.

MISS BRAHMS 'Ere have you been showing him your knickers?

MRS SLOCOMBE That'll do, Miss Brahms. I'm afraid the garment you refer to is not available.

PEACOCK Why not?

MRS SLOCOMBE It's gone to the laundry.

There is more firing.

HUMPHRIES When's the laundry come back?

PEACOCK We must let them know we're here somehow.

LUCAS Wave your bowler hat at them.

PEACOCK You may have something there, Mr Lucas. Someone wearing a bowler hat could probably draw their attention and address them over the wall. Mr Rumbold has a hat.

RUMBOLD You can borrow it with pleasure.

During the following, **LUCAS** *goes to* **RUMBOLD***'s tent.*

PEACOCK May I remind you, sir, that only management are allowed to wear bowler hats.

RUMBOLD I could over-rule that decision.

PEACOCK I wouldn't hear of it, sir.

LUCAS *returns with the bowler hat and hands it to* **RUMBOLD.**

LUCAS Good luck, Mr Rumbold.

RUMBOLD *takes the hat.*

RUMBOLD What shall I say?

MRS SLOCOMBE Just tell them we're British and they're spoiling our holiday.

HUMPHRIES And say there's a sister of mercy here that's got to get back to the nunnery to hold her canticles.

RUMBOLD *turns to the wall.*

GRAINGER This is just the sort of thing that made Britain great.

RUMBOLD *mounts a brick step and looks over the wall.*

RUMBOLD Now look here you lot.

There is a burst of fire. His hat is shot off. He comes back and sits down.

I don't think that was a very good idea, Peacock.

GRAINGER Why don't we phone the British Embassy?

PEACOCK Good idea.

They ring the bell for service.

BERNARDO *enters.*

Bernardo—telephone the British Embassy and tell them we're here.

BERNARDO I cannot, sir, we're cut off.

PEACOCK Can you take a message?

BERNARDO No, señor. No man is safe on the streets.

LUCAS In that case, let's send Mr Humphries.

HUMPHRIES I'll slap your wrist in a minute.

LUCAS I'm not being funny. You're dressed as a nun—your habit could save you.

HUMPHRIES That'll be a change.

PEACOCK I'm sure you could do it, Mr Humphries.

HUMPHRIES I'm not budging.

MRS SLOCOMBE Couldn't we send a message some other way?

MISS BRAHMS I'm reading a book where they put a note in a bottle. Mind you, they were on a desert island—and it did take three years.

HUMPHRIES *(pointing up)* The answer is there. Up above.

PEACOCK Mr Humphries, don't get carried away by your costume.

HUMPHRIES I'm not—I'm talking about the balloon. All we've got to do is pull it down, write a message on the table cloth and tie it on.

MRS SLOCOMBE Oh, isn't that ingenious.

PEACOCK Quick, Mr Lucas—wind down the balloon.

LUCAS Very good, Captain Peacock.

During the ensuing dialogue LUCAS *winds down the balloon. The bottom of the balloon comes into view. There is an anchor trailing and the banner dangling advertising the hotel.*

MRS SLOCOMBE Come on, Miss Brahms—get the things off the cloth.

MISS BRAHMS What are we going to write with?

PEACOCK Has anyone got a lipstick?

HUMPHRIES Don't look at me. We're not allowed to wear any.

MRS SLOCOMBE Here we are.

MISS BRAHMS I've got one too.

MRS SLOCOMBE What shall we write?

RUMBOLD Please inform British Consul General that Grace Brothers executive trapped in this hotel.

PEACOCK We haven't time for all that. Just put "Help—British".

MRS SLOCOMBE I'll write Help—you write British.

CESAR enters, blood-stained and bandaged. DON BERNARDO and CONCHITA also enter.

CESAR It's no good, all is lost.

BERNARDO Please, Cesar—surrender.

CESAR Never—Cesar will never surrender to those imperial pigs.

CONCHITA But they are bringing up the big cannons.

BERNARDO And there are more planes coming—look.

Jets are heard again.

CONCHITA You must surrender, Cesar.

BERNARDO Leave us and save us. They will blow up my beautiful hotel.

CESAR Never, I will never surrender.

MRS SLOCOMBE *(kneeling)* But please, Cesar. At least let the women go free.

HUMPHRIES Yes, think of us women. And the babies.

CESAR I see no babies.

HUMPHRIES I'm going to have one in a minute.

During this PEACOCK *and* RUMBOLD *take the cloth and pin it to the hotel sign under the balloons. Sound of jets diving again.*

PEACOCK Take care—they might open fire.

MRS SLOCOMBE Where can we go?

LUCAS *(pointing to the loo)* In there—it's got a corrugated roof.

CESAR Then I will go in there.

He beats MRS SLOCOMBE *to the loo.*

MISS BRAHMS Quick, while he's in there—bolt him in.

The plane machine guns are heard. Ornaments on the wall fall off.

PEACOCK Get the balloon up before it's too late.

RUMBOLD Take the brake off.

LUCAS *does so. The balloon and the sign rise. The anchor catches by a trick line under the roof of the loo. The loo rises in the air with yells from* CESAR. *(We suggest that* CESAR *hides in a trap in rostrum under the loo) Sound of gunfire.*

PEACOCK They're firing at him.

RUMBOLD He's surrendering.

LUCAS What's he waving?

The gunfire stops.

PEACOCK Whatever it is, they've stopped firing.

LUCAS He's dropped it.

MRS SLOCOMBE's *Union Jack knickers flutter down.*

PEACOCK Mrs Slocombe, your knickers.

MISS BRAHMS How did he get them?

PEACOCK *sings the first line of "AH SWEET MYSTERY".*

MRS SLOCOMBE There's dozens of them about—they were in Kendal Milne's sale.

HUMPHRIES You're quite right. *(He lifts his habit to show that he too is wearing a pair)*

The others continue to sing "AH SWEET MYSTERY", etc.

Curtain.

FURNITURE AND PROPERTY LIST

Further dressing may be added at the director's discretion

ACT I

On stage:　2 lifts with buttons etc., one malfunctioning
Gentlemen's counter. *On it:* pad and pencil, phone, chalk
Ladies' counter. *On it:* sign in book, pen, tape measure, chalk. *In drawer:* underwear display
Girl model with flimsy nightdress with fur hem
Girl model in skirt, blouse and pair of knickers loosely attached
Chair
Pair of gloves on display
Umbrella
Male dummy wearing wool bathing shorts
Heavy-handled walking stick

Offstage:　Bucket with water and sponge, vacuum cleaner (**Mash**)
Suitcase (**Miss Brahms**)
2 suitcases (**Peacock**)
Golf clubs (**Mash**)
Cat basket (**Mrs Slocombe**)
Feather duster (**Mash**)
Crate containing **Humphries** (**Mash**)
Huge syringe (**Nurse**)
Clockwork false teeth (**Lucas**)
Flask of brandy (**Mrs Slocombe**)
Trolley containing German signs (**Mash**)
4 boxes containing bras, large canvas bra, socks, pair of long johns (**Mash**)
Squeeze-box (**Rumbold**)
Flask (**Mrs Slocombe**)
Wheelchair (**Mr Grace**)

Miss Brahms: large duffle bag
Lucas: plaster cast wrapped round Wellington boot, three pencils in breast pocket
Mrs Slocombe: passport containing sexy picture
Humphries: wrist-watch, handbag, tape measure
Male Customer: spectacle case
Mrs Slocombe: glasses
Peacock: glasses, carnation in buttonhole
Rumbold: list of figures
Mash: Hindenberg helmet

ACT II

On stage: Don Bernardo Hotel Reception:
Reception counter. *On it:* phone, bell, book
Large illustration of annexe
Bolt

Tent Area:
7 tents containing Lilos and beds, etc.
Outdoor loo
Winding handle connected to rope going up
Pile of chairs

Offstage: 2 balloons with "Hotel Don Bernardo" signs (**Mrs Slocombe**)
2 balloons with "Hotel Don Bernardo" signs (**Miss Brahms**)
Long balloon (**Humphries**)
Mrs Slocombe's wig on ventriloquist dummy (**Lucas**)
Cases and passports, **Mrs Slocombe's** containing picture (**All Brits**)
Table on wheels. *On it:* table cloth, dishes and bowls of food, crockery and cutlery, giant lobster in lidded dish, octopus in dish, long bread rolls, napkins, glasses, etc. (**Conchita**)
Spanish wine jug, big goblet (**Bernardo**)
Handbag containing pencil, mirror, lipstick (**Miss Brahms**)

Personal: **Humphries**: mirror, comb (carried throughout)
           Cesar: gun
           Grainger: pair of scissors
           Peacock: phrase book, pen
           Lucas: pencil
           Miss Brahms: sunglasses

During Black-out on page 53

Set: Don Bernardo Hotel Reception
           Sexy photo of **Mrs Slocombe**
           Bottle
           2 glasses

Personal: **Humphries**: wallet
           Bernard: bottle of aftershave

During front of tabs action leading up to Black-out on page 56

Set: **Miss Brahms**'s book
           Mrs Slocombe's make-up box, containing perfume
               spray and bottles, large bottle of Badedas, wig
               and dress or wrap, balloons
           Peacock's electric shaver
           Peacock's aftershave
           Humphries' sponge bag
           Humphries' hairdrier
           Large caterpillar type woof-n-poofs
           Fly swatter
           Dressing-gown

Offstage: Sponge bag (**Grainger**)
           Mrs Slocombe's sexy photo (**Cesar**)
           2 burst balloons (**Cesar**)

Personal: **Humphries**: hair curlers
           Mrs Slocombe: note
           Bernardo: bolt
           Cesar: dagger

During Black-out on page 70

Set: Don Bernardo Hotel Reception
    Table set for breakfast with croissants, etc.
    Hotel balloon with hotel banner
    Miss Brahms's transistor
    Rumbold's bowler hat
    Mrs Slocombe's Union Jack knickers in loo

Offstage: Tray piled with eggs, bacon, toast and marmalade,
    coffee (Conchita)

Personal: **Rumbold**: large beaknose nose shade

LIGHTING PLOT

Property fittings required: nil
2 interior and 1 exterior settings

ACT I

To open: Overall general lighting

No cues

ACT II

To open: Overall general lighting

Cue 1	**Bernardo:** "I give her to you."	(Page 42)
	Cross-fade to walled patio	
Cue 2	**Humphries:** "That should dampen his ardour."	(Page 53)
	Black-out	
Cue 3	**ASM** set Reception scene	(Page 54)
	Bring up overall lighting	
Cue 4	**Cesar** kisses photo	(Page 56)
	Black-out	
Cue 5	**Grainger**'s voice is heard singing	(Page 56)
	Bring up night lighting on tents	
Cue 6	**Peacock** switches his light out	(Page 59)
	Cut lighting to light in **Miss Brahms's** *tent only*	
Cue 7	**Miss Brahms** bangs on tent with fly swatter	(Page 59)
	Turn on **Humphries'** *light*	
Cue 8	**Miss Brahms** turns light out	(Page 60)
	Cut **Miss Brahms's** *light*	

EFFECTS PLOT

ACT I

Cue 1   **Mrs Slocombe**: "…couldn't open the
door for letters."   (Page 12)
Store bell rings

Cue 2   **Peacock** exits   (Page 22)
Lift bell dings

Cue 3   **All** go into a huddle   (Page 28)
*Joke teeth start to move inside model's
trunks*

Cue 4   **Lucas** starts to walk towards model   (Page 28)
Teeth stop

Cue 5   **Miss Brahms** crosses   (Page 28)
Teeth start again

Cue 6   **Miss Brahms** stops dead   (Page 28)
Teeth stop

Cue 7   **Mrs Slocombe** puts her glasses on   (Page 28)
Teeth start again

Cue 8   **Mrs Slocombe** looks again   (Page 28)
Teeth stop

Cue 9   **Peacock** takes his glasses off and
is about to turn away   (Page 28)
Teeth start again and stop in a while

Cue 10   **Humphries** moves towards model   (Page 28)
Teeth start again

Cue 11   **Humphries** grabs hold of **Peacock**'s
hand   (Page 28)
Teeth stop

Cue 12   **Humphries** stretches out a tentative
hand   (Page 28)
Teeth start again

Bell on table rings offstage

Cue 25 Grainger: "I shan't stray very far from
       the hotel."   (Page 74)
      Gun shot off

Cue 26 **Peacock**: "Probably a shooting party."   (Page 75)
      More shots

Cue 27 **Peacock**: "You get them anywhere."   (Page 75)
      *Sound of plane diving and machine
       gun burst*

Cue 28 **Mrs Slocombe**: "...go after them with
      jet planes."   (Page 75)
      More shots off

Cue 29 **Miss Brahms** turns on her transistor   (Page 76)
      *Radio squeaks few times, few snatches
       in foreign language, then BBC Voice,
       followed by burst of machine gunfire
       and decorations and architectural
       features falling off wall above doors
       and windows*

Cue 30 **Mrs Slocombe**: "It's gone to the laundry." (Page 76)
      Sound of more firing

Cue 31 **Rumbold**: "Now look here you lot."   (Page 77)
      Burst of gunfire, **Rumbold***'s hat is shot
       off*

Cue 32 **Bernardo**: "...more planes coming—look."   (Page 79)
      Sound of jets

Cue 33 **Humphries**: "I'm going to have one in
      a minute."   (Page 80)
      Sound of jets diving

Cue 34 **Miss Brahms**: "...he's in there—bolt
      him in."   (Page 80)
      *Sound of plane machine guns,
       ornaments fall off wall*

VISIT THE SAMUEL FRENCH BOOKSHOP AT THE ROYAL COURT THEATRE

Browse plays and theatre books, get expert advice and enjoy a coffee

Samuel French Bookshop
Royal Court Theatre
Sloane Square
London
SW1W 8AS
020 7565 5024

Shop from thousands of titles on our website

 samuelfrench.co.uk

 samuelfrenchltd

 samuel french uk

Lightning Source UK Ltd.
Milton Keynes UK
UKHW022149260919
350509UK00007B/351/P